GILBY'S GUNS

On the dark night when Frank Gilby shot at a man coming out of the alley near the bank, he didn't realize that it was his wife's lover until it was too late. Gilby and his wife split up and went their separate ways. Looking for work, Gilby would have been lynched as a rustler if Helena Goodnight and the boys from the Flying G hadn't saved him. The mayor gave Gilby the job of sheriff and his first task was to go after the rustlers who plagued the range. But he was going to face death many times before the dust finally settled . . .

H. H. CODY

GILBY'S GUNS

Complete and Unabridged

LINFORD
Leicester

First published in Great Britain in 2003 by
Robert Hale Limited
London

First Linford Edition
published 2004
by arrangement with
Robert Hale Limited
London

British Library CIP Data

Cody, H. H.
   Gilby's guns.—Large print ed.—
Linford western library
1. Western stories
2. Large type books
I. Title
823.9'14 [F]

ISBN 1–84395–378–1

Published by
F. A. Thorpe (Publishing)
Anstey, Leicestershire

Set by Words & Graphics Ltd.
Anstey, Leicestershire
Printed and bound in Great Britain by
T. J. International Ltd., Padstow, Cornwall

This book is printed on acid-free paper

1

Sheriff Frank Gilby stood at the door of his office watching the street for any sign of Mercy, his wife, coming in his direction. For the second time that week she was late, he thought, in a disgruntled way, as he went back into the office and closed the door. It wasn't like her. Mercy was usually pretty prompt in coming down to his office with something to eat when he was on the night shift. Maybe it was the fact that he hadn't had such a great day. Ben, his deputy, had been shot in the back by a drunken gambler that afternoon, and the fella who ran the Wells Fargo office had skipped with the contents of the safe and left no forwarding address.

Against all his own rules he took a bottle from the desk drawer and pulled the cork. He took one swallow and put it away. He felt relieved when the door opened and Mercy came in holding a basket with his food in it.

She gave him a sweet smile and put it on the desk in front of him.

'Enjoy your supper,' she said, moving back towards the door.

'Hey,' he said getting up quickly. 'Ain't you got time to stay awhile?'

'Sorry Frank, not tonight,' she said laughing, and playfully pushing him away.

'What's the matter?' he asked her. 'You've usually got time for a kiss.'

'Not tonight, Frank,' she said, putting a little more force into the push.

Gilby moved away from her. What was the matter with her these days? Usually she was more than happy to spend a little time in the office with him, providing there were no prisoners in the cells and tonight there were no prisoners in the cells.

'Have I upset you?' he asked her, putting his hand on the door handle.

'No, of course not, silly.' she said,

with a grin that wasn't exactly genuine.

Gilby felt puzzled. Something was the matter.

'Come on, Mercy,' he said. 'What is it?'

'Nothing, Frank, I've already told you.' Mercy's voice suddenly became very defensive. 'Now, I've got to get back home.'

'See you tomorrow,' Gilby said, as she went out.

'Yes, see you, Frank,' she said, hurrying away in the direction of the bank.

Gilby was about to call out to her that she was going the wrong way, but she had already disappeared into the dark. He closed the door and went over to the desk. A cloth covered the basket. He took it off. Whatever was in there sure smelled good.

Gilby sat down to eat. The potatoes and vegetables were good but the pie was even better. He finished up with a feeling of satisfaction. Mercy had put a pot of fresh coffee in with the food.

Gilby poured some and drank it. Something didn't figure, he thought, as he swallowed the coffee Something was sure wrong with Mercy this last couple of weeks, but he couldn't figure what.

He got up and walked round the office, just to stretch his limbs. On the wall, the clock said it was still half an hour before he went on his rounds. With a sudden burst of restless energy he pulled his .45 and checked the loads. He'd do his rounds half an hour earlier. Maybe that would make him feel better.

The street was quiet as Gilby walked down it. The only real noise was coming from the Fair Lady saloon. A trail crew that had been taking a herd up north had come in late that afternoon and was going to make sure that it drank all the dust out of its throat, and spent some dinero with the soiled doves in the saloons.

Gilby decided to take a look inside and make sure things were all right. Trail crews were a pretty rowdy lot who tended to get out of hand fairly quickly and stay out of hand. As he got to the door of the saloon, a couple of shots slammed into the wood.

Gilby drew his .45 and pushed the doors open. A sudden silence had fallen on the place. Two men stood in the middle of the room. One, by his clothes, must have come in with the trail crew. He was holding a smoking gun. The other fella was the house gambler. Suddenly, the gambler twisted, clutching his belly, his face contorted with pain and fell to the sawdust-covered floor.

'You got the bastard,' one of the cowboys yelled triumphantly.

The rest of the trail crew yelled their approval.

'Be quiet,' Gilby shouted, firing into the ceiling. 'Drop the gun,' he said to the cowboy.

Opening his hand the cowboy let the .45 fall to the floor.

'Did you do this?' Gilby indicated the bleeding body on the floor.

'It didn't do itself,' Clem Wyburn, the

ramrod of the crew laughed. 'Did it, Jacko?'

'He had more cards up his sleeve, than there was in the deck,' Jacko said, a grin on his swarthy face.

'I didn't ask you that,' Gilby told him.

'Everybody in the place could see him drawing cards out of his sleeve,' Jacko Williams, the toughest member of the crew outside Clem Wyburn replied, with a wide, toothy grin.

'Like hell he was.' Calum Stirzaker, the owner of the saloon stepped forward. 'We run a clean game in this house.'

Stirzaker was a big man, with broad shoulders, and a fat cigar hanging out of his mouth, his thumb stuck in his suspenders. The fingers that he wrapped round the cigar were even fatter and on one he sported a ring with a blue diamond in it. He took the cigar out of his mouth and tapped it against the bar. He crossed the saloon floor, stepping over the gambler's body. His and Gilby's faces were within an inch or two of each other.

'I know all about your clean games. This is the third shooting this month, and always it's been the same gambler who's ended up with a corpse at his feet. Seems like he's run out of luck this time. One more shooting and I'll close you down and run you out of town.'

'My fella wasn't cheating,' Stirzaker answered.

'Sure he was,' Clem Wyburn chipped in. 'Everybody in the place knows it.'

Stirzaker rounded on him.

'There's always trouble when you fellas come through town,' a customer at the bar said.

'Yer damn quick to take our money,' said one of the trail crew. 'Money we've worked damned hard to earn.'

'An' you're damn quick to gamble it away,' shouted one of the customers.

The two parties started to separate and line up on either side of the room. Gilby fired a shot into the air as the whole thing threatened to turn into a riot.

'That's enough,' he shouted. 'You, down to the jail.'

Jacko tossed Gilby a hard look. Reluctantly, the rest of the trail crew got out of Gilby's way as he walked to the door. Suddenly, the ramrod of the crew made a dive for his gun. Gilby fired; Clem Wyburn dropped the gun and rubbed his hand. One of his men came forward and gave him his bandanna to wrap round it.

'Thanks,' the ramrod mumbled.

'It'll sting for a bit, but there's no real harm done,' Gilby told him. 'If you do it again, I'll take one of your fingers off.'

Jacko made a lunge for the door, but Gilby kicked his legs from under him.

'Forget it,' Gilby told him, and waggled his gun in the direction of the jail.

Jacko started to move, a scowl on his face. A handful of people watched Gilby take his prisoner down to the jail. Once there, Gilby pushed him into the cell and locked the door behind him.

2

Taking a shotgun down from the rack, Gilby thumbed a couple of shells into it. He had the feeling that the night wasn't over. A few minutes later he saw a gang of men coming down the street from the direction of the saloon. As they got to the end of the street another group came out from another direction. Gilby spat onto the sidewalk. A group of cowboys and a mob from the saloon. They met head on. As he ran down towards them the fighting started. For a moment he stood on the edge of it. He didn't want to fire the shotgun into them. Looking round he saw his answer.

'Lemmy,' he called out to the owner of the livery.

Lemmy Bridges watched the brawling for a minute, his face white. Then Gilby called him over again.

'Yeah, what is it, Frank? he asked the sheriff, over the commotion.

'You got these fella's horses in there?' Gilby said, indicating the livery stable.

'Yeah, half a dozen. You gonna stampede them into this mob?' Lemmy asked him with a grin.

'Sure, I figure they'll do less damage than a couple of barrels of buckshot,' Gilby answered him. 'These fellas know the value of a good horse and they don't want to lose them.'

'You might be right,' Lemmy laughed, heading towards the livery.

They ran into the livery and started to get the horses out of their stalls. Outside the sound of the brawling became even louder and people came out onto the street to watch it.

Clem Wyburn and a couple of townsmen were going at it with planks of wood, their faces and heads cut and covered with blood. Half a dozen other cowboys and townsmen were rolling about in the dust, snarling and kicking at each other.

'Sure hope this works,' Lemmy said, holding the leathers of the horses.

'So do I,' Gilby replied, putting the shotgun down on the boardwalk, drawing his .45 and firing a shot into the air.

The horses stampeded towards the mêlée. Straightaway it broke up and the mob scrambled out of the way. The ramrod and his two assailants broke up their fight.

'What the hell do you think you're doing?' Clem Wyburn yelled, running towards Gilby. 'We've got to round them horses up, if we can find them.'

'My heart bleeds for you,' Gilby told him, putting away his gun. 'Now, get after them.'

Bending down he picked up the shotgun. He could see that the ramrod hadn't had enough. Stepping onto the boardwalk he tossed the shotgun to an onlooker. Clem Wyburn balled his fists and came at him. Gilby parried the punch and sent one into the ramrod's already bleeding head.

The ramrod staggered under the blow, but came back again.

'Yer a tough son-of-a-bitch,' Gilby said grudgingly.

'Tough enough to take you,' Wyburn said, through his bloodied and smashed lips. Balling his fists, he came at Gilby again.

They traded blows for a while as the townsfolk looked on, cheering for Gilby. The trail crew formed a semi-circle round the two men, and cheered their trail boss on. Gilby could see that the man had a hell of a capacity to take punishment. He tossed a double-hander into the trail boss's face. It went up like a stick of dynamite on his nose, breaking it, and sending out a spray of blood, that covered Gilby as well.

'Ain't you ever had enough?' Gilby asked the man, as he reeled under the blow.

Steadying himself and shaking off the pain, the trail boss came at Gilby again.

'There ain't enough,' he called over to Gilby, with a hard laugh.

'Damn it, quit, I don't want to kill you,' Gilby told him.

'You ain't the man to kill me,' the ramrod shouted, wiping his mashed lips.

'I sure as hell hope I don't have to,' Gilby balanced himself on his legs and waited for the ramrod's onslaught.

It came hard and fast, and Gilby had to ride a succession of blows that left him reeling. When the man drew back, Gilby balanced himself again. He parried the incoming blow, and drew himself up to send in the killer punch knowing that at last the ramrod was tiring.

When the ramrod took a step back, Gilby punched him in the midriff. His opponent let out a gasp as the air left his lungs. As he doubled up, Gilby finished him with an uppercut that sent him reeling back across the street. The ramrod lay in the dirt, not moving. To Gilby's surprise, the trail crew clapped and cheered him, and tossed their hats into the air.

'OK,' Gilby said. 'Get him cleaned up and get your horses found. Then tell him when he comes round, his boy's staying in jail until I get to the bottom of this shooting.'

They got his body picked up and threw a hatful of water from the trough into his face. He came round like the wreck of a battered ship that had just weathered a hell of a storm.

'What hit me?' he asked one of his men.

'That's what hit you,' the man said, pointing to Gilby who was walking to his office.

'Throws a hell of a punch,' the trail boss muttered, rubbing his jaw and getting unsteadily to his feet.

Opening up the office, Gilby took the bottle from his desk and poured a big drink into his mug. He tossed it down in one. Sitting with his head back, he let the fire settle in his stomach.

When it had burned itself out, he filled the bowl with some water from the bucket back where the cells were, and cleaned off his face. Then for a while he sat at his desk.

Gilby went to the door of his office. Once again the street was empty.

He wondered where Mercy was. Maybe she had come back down to the jail while he had been in the saloon, or out on the street calming down the fight, but somehow he didn't think she had. Something was starting to bite him. It wasn't like Mercy not to show up, but this was the third time in two weeks that she hadn't come down to the office with some more grub for him. He pulled the door closed behind him and locked it, then started off down the boardwalk, hefting his gun. As Gilby walked past the bank, he heard a scuffling noise from inside the alley. His hand dropped to his gun, and he drew it from the leather.

'What's going on down there?' Gilby called out. 'This is the sheriff.'

As the words left his mouth, two figures ran from the alley.

'Stand still,' he called after them,

drawing back the hammer on his gun.

The two figures kept on running.

'Stand still,' he called out again. They kept on running.

Gilby fired at the fleeing figures, and saw the bullet kick the rear figure into the horse trough outside the saloon. The water splashed over the edge of the trough. The other figure stopped running and screamed loudly, leaning against the saloon wall. Running up to them, Gilby saw that the figure leaning on the wall of the saloon, her hand to her mouth, was Mercy. The bleeding figure in the trough was Roy Carson, the bank manager's son.

People were starting to come out of the saloon.

'What's going on?' the owner of the Bright Star saloon asked Gilby.

He stopped short when he saw who was lying in the trough, and Gilby holstering his gun.

'What the hell have you done, Sheriff?' he demanded. 'There's going to be hell to pay for this.'

Frank turned to look at Mercy. 'What were you doing in that alley?' he asked her.

'What most cats do down alleys,' the saloon owner said.

The crowd started to laugh until they realized that it was the sheriff's wife.

'What were you doing in that alley?' an angry Gilby demanded, grabbing Mercy by the arm.

She returned his gaze, and shook her head.

'Get the undertaker,' Gilby said, to the fella who owned the saloon.

'Sure thing, Sheriff,' he said with a shaky laugh.

As he walked away, Gilby took hold of Mercy's arm and led her towards the jail.

He unlocked the door and pushed her inside.

'Just what were you doing coming out of that alley?' he demanded again.

'We'd just come out of the bank by the side entrance, and Roy panicked when he heard you. Isn't it obvious what we were doing in the bank?'

'No, I don't understand,' he said quietly. 'The bank was closed, you had no business being in there,' Gilby said, unable to take in what Mercy had said to him.

'Frank,' she tried again.

It suddenly became clear to Gilby what had been going on in the bank.

'Mercy,' he said, his face taking on a look of rage.

'For God's sake, Frank. You were never going to be more than a hick town sheriff. I wanted more. There's got to be more in the world than this place,' she exclaimed, gesturing around the office.

'Mercy,' Gilby shouted.

'Take a good look, Frank. You're never going to amount to anything in this town. I've had enough. And it looks like you've killed the man who could have helped me to become something.'

Her outburst had come as a shock to Gilby.

'How come you never said anything

about this to me?'

'There wouldn't be any point, Frank,' she said. 'You've got what you want, a shiny tin star and a town to wear it in.'

Gilby stiffened when she said this. 'I thought that was what you wanted,' he said, with a mixture of anger and surprise.

'You think I wanted just this, Frank? If you did you are a bigger fool than I thought you were,' she snapped suddenly.

'I really made a mistake with you,' he blazed out angrily.

'Something we all do from time to time,' Mercy said, suddenly becoming cool.

Frank pushed her away from him. 'You make me sick,' he said, his head dropping into his hands.

'I'm sorry you feel that way,' Mercy told him. 'I guess that means it's all over.'

'You guess right,' he said in a low voice, his fists clenching and unclenching on the desk.

'Mind if I go home now?' she asked, moving away from him.

'No, I don't mind,' he said in a weary voice.

Frank watched as she walked out of the office. She closed the door quietly behind her. Gilby hit the wall with his clenched fist, and swore under his breath. He had known Mercy for a while and had not realized that this was not the kind of life that she wanted, but it was her relationship with Roy Carson that stuck in his throat. He had figured from the first that he could trust her.

3

The next morning Carson's old man came storming into Gilby's office.

'What's this about you shooting my boy?' he demanded, his beefy face red with rage.

Gilby stood up. 'I saw two people coming out of the alley beside the bank,' Gilby told him.

'So?' Carson demanded.

'I told them to stop and they ignored me.'

'So you shot him down.' Carson's old man slammed his fist on the desk.

'For God's sake,' Gilby said. 'What was I supposed to do? I shouted a warning. They knew the sheriff was coming.'

'And who was the other fella?'

'My wife.' Gilby stared into Jim Carson's face. 'My wife had been having an affair behind my back with your son.'

'That was no reason to shoot him,' the old man yelled at Gilby.

Gilby was starting to wonder if Carson thought he had shot his son on purpose.

'I didn't shoot him because he was in the bank with my wife, I shot him because he came out of the alley and just kept on running when I told him to stop.'

'You shot Roy because he was having an affair with your wife, didn't you?' Carson ranted on.

Gilby was on the edge of losing his temper.

'That's crazy talk. I shot your son because he came running out of the alley beside the bank. Not because he was having affair with my wife. If I had, I would have settled it with him and her face to face. I wouldn't have shot him in the back.'

'So you say.' Old man Carson leaned across the desk, his face getting redder and redder. The sweat oozed out of his pores.

Snatching at his lapel, Gilby dragged Carson towards him.

'Like I said, I shot your son when I saw him coming out of the alley and he wouldn't stop when I told him to.'

The old man suddenly stopped struggling in Gilby's arms and went limp.

Easing him back across the desk, Gilby lowered him to the floor and took a good look at him.

'Damn it,' he swore to himself.

Quickly he went into the street and grabbed Gus Roberts, the owner of the general store.

'Get the doc up here,' he told him.

Roberts ran down the street in the direction of the doctor's office. Back inside, Gilby found Carson still breathing but making hard work of it.

'Ease up,' he said to the old man. 'The doc will soon be here.'

Carson turned his head away from

Gilby and looked at the wall, saying nothing.

'He's had a seizure,' Doc Grissom said, after he had examined the old man. 'Best get him back to my place and get his wife out here.'

They got Carson down to Grissom's place and sent out to his house for his wife.

Celia Carson came to the office twenty minutes later. She was a white-haired woman in her fifties with a thin face.

'I got your message,' she said to Grissom, when she hurried in the door. 'How is he?'

Grissom followed her into his surgery.

'He ain't too bad, just a mild seizure,' he told her, rinsing his hands in a bowl of water.

'Did somebody try to rob the bank?' she asked, as soon as she saw Gilby.

'No,' Gilby started to say, then he realized that she did not know about her son's death.

'What is it?' she asked, seeing the look on his face.

'Roy's dead,' Gilby told her quickly. 'I shot him.'

'Dead?' she echoed, her eyes widening and her mouth dropping open.

Gilby repeated what had happened earlier that night.

'You shot Roy? You blundering fool,' she screamed hysterically, beating at his chest.

'It was an accident. He shouldn't have been in the bank,' Gilby said defensively, as he pushed her away.

'For God's sake, what was he doing in the bank at that time of the night?'

'I've got my patient to worry about,' Grissom said, easing them both out into his living room.

'My son wouldn't do a thing like that,' she yelled at Gilby when he had told her what had happened. 'He wouldn't. He's a well-brought-up boy.'

'You can take my word for it that he did. Ask Mercy, she's at home now.'

'I still don't believe it. Roy's a good

boy. He just wouldn't do a thing like that,' she went on, her anger abating a little.

'Like I said, go and ask Mercy if you want to,' Gilby said to her.

With a look of anger on her thin face, Celia Carson stormed out of the house.

A few minutes later Doc Grissom came back.

'How is he?' Gilby asked him.

'Not too bad. The best thing he can get is some rest. From the look of you, you look as though you could do with some rest yourself. You've had a busy night from what I hear.'

'Hell, I almost forgot my prisoner,' Gilby said quickly.

He hurried down to the jail. A crowd was gathering outside.

'What's going on?' he demanded.

'We've just come to string up the sidewinder who shot the gambler,' came a reply from the front of the mob. Gilby recognized him as one of Stirzaker's barkeeps.

'Nobody's going to do any stringing

up while I'm sheriff here,' Gilby said firmly, drawing his .45.

'We are, Sheriff,' the same fella said, taking a step forward. 'Maybe you won't be sheriff for much longer.'

Gilby saw the noose in his hands. 'Stay where you are,' he told the mob.

'You can't shoot all of us,' the barkeep said.

'That's true,' Gilby answered. 'But I can get you first, then four of your friends.'

The barkeep hesitated, the noose almost slipping out of his hands.

'Are you coming for him or not?' Gilby asked them, his hand curling round his gun.

The barkeep dropped the noose and started to move away. One at a time, the rest of the mob followed him.

'Didn't think you'd risk it,' Gilby said, his hands moving away from his gun butt.

With the street quiet again, Gilby went back into his office and checked on his prisoner. By that time it was getting on towards daylight and the sky was colouring up in the east. Not having the heart to go home, Gilby laid his head on the desk and closed his eyes for a spell. The next thing he remembered was being shaken awake.

Will Forrester, the mayor, was standing over him, looking pretty grim.

'Just come from Grissom's place. Jim Carson's in there. He's picking up, but it's gonna be a long job,' he said.

Standing up, Gilby stretched. 'Guess you know what happened?' he asked Forrester.

Forrester shrugged. 'I've heard his side of it, but I ain't heard yours.'

Again Gilby repeated the events of the night. Forrester shrugged once more.

'What happened between old man Carson's boy and your wife ain't any of my concern. The old man thinks you shot Roy on purpose.'

'That's a damned lie,' Gilby exploded.

'I know you well enough to believe you,' Forrester said. 'But Carson's word carries a lot of weight in this town.'

'I know that,' Gilby snapped. 'So what are you saying?'

'I'm saying you should go home and talk to Mercy. Try and sort things out. I'll keep an eye on things here, and think about getting a new deputy.'

'OK, see you later,' Gilby said.

People who had heard about the shooting at the bank, eyed him with a mixture of curiosity and pity as he walked home.

They had a house on the edge of town, one that Gilby had had built just before he and Mercy had got married. He pushed open the gate and walked down the path. Hesitating for a moment, he waited, then put the key in the lock. He deliberately slammed it hard just to let Mercy know that he was back. He walked down the hall and went into the sitting-room. Mercy was sitting by the window. She did not look up at him.

'I suppose you want an explanation,' she said.

'I thought you made it pretty clear a few hours ago,' he said angrily.

'It's all over, Frank, like you said. This isn't what I wanted,' she said, looking round.

'You should have thought of that before you and Carson started on it,' he snarled.

A look of helplessness and loss crossed her face.

For a moment Gilby felt sorry for her, then he remembered the bullet that had flung Roy Carson into the trough, and the look on Forrester's face. He knew that he couldn't stay as sheriff in this town any longer. Mercy seemed to sense that something was going to happen.

'What will you do?' she asked him.

'Move on, I suppose, and you?'

She shrugged. 'Like you, I can't stay here. I'll start packing.'

'Me, too,' he said.

The morning found Gilby feeling pretty lousy. Mercy had called in earlier on with her case packed ready to get the stage. From his office door Gilby watched her walk down the street and wait outside the Wells Fargo office.

He went back inside and pushed the door closed. For a moment he stood over his desk and opened the drawer. His hand hovered over the whiskey bottle. Then, forcefully, he pushed it closed. He looked up at the clock. Nine o'clock, time to do his morning rounds.

Outside, the sun was hot and he knew that it was going to be a scorcher of a day. The people he met greeted him as if they knew that Mercy had left. On the boardwalk outside Gus Roberts's place, Stirzaker stood in front of him as he walked down the street, a grin of twisted satisfaction on his face.

'Saw Mercy heading down to the Wells Fargo office with her bag. Is she going away or something?'

'You know damn well she's going,' Gilby told him, feeling his anger rise.

Stirzaker took the cigar out of his mouth and flicked the ash towards Gilby. The slight breeze carried some of the ash into Gilby's face.

'Sorry about that, sheriff,' Stirzaker sneered, taking a silk handkerchief from his pocket.

Gilby pushed the hand away as he offered it.

'Take it easy, Sheriff,' Stirzaker said, in a voice loud enough to be heard by those nearby.

One or two people looked round at them.

'Keep yer damned handkerchief to yerself,' Gilby snarled, realizing that Stirzaker was doing his best to anger him.

'No need to take that tone, Sheriff,' Stirzaker continued. 'Only trying to be helpful,' he said, in a voice that was just short of a sneer.

'Damn you and your helpfulness,' Gilby said, as he tried to pass by.

Stirzaker pushed out a leg which caused Gilby to stumble. He caught Gilby as if to prevent him falling.

'Keep yer hands off me,' Gilby shouted at him.

Those on the boardwalk turned to watch the two men.

'Like I said, Sheriff, I was only trying to be helpful,' Stirzaker said, an oily grin on his face.

'I know what you were trying to do,' Gilby snapped at him.

'Go easy, Sheriff,' one of the barkeeps from Stirzaker's saloon put in. 'The boss is right. He was just trying to help.'

'Like hell your boss was trying to help,' Gilby snarled at the barkeep. 'I know just what your boss was trying to do.'

'The hell with you,' Stirzaker said, coming to stand beside his barkeep. 'You're just sore because of the trouble in the saloon last night. You're just trying to find an excuse to close me down.'

'If I wanted to close you down I'd just come and do it,' Gilby told him.

A crowd was gathering round the argument.

'Come on, Sheriff,' Stirzaker said. 'You're just blowing a little trouble up out of all proportion. Ain't that right, Barney?'

'Sure is, boss,' put in the barkeep. 'Just a little misunderstanding over a hand of cards.'

'I don't call three shootings over a deck of cards a misunderstanding: I call it calculated cheating,' Gilby told them both.

Stirzaker shrugged. 'Maybe we just see things differently,' he said.

'Maybe we'd just better start seeing things in the same way from now on,' Gilby said, finishing the conversation and walking away.

Behind him he heard the people break into a buzz of conversation.

Forrester came to see him later.

'Can't seem to get a replacement deputy for Ben,' he said, putting his foot on the chair opposite Gilby. 'Your run in with Stirzaker didn't help much.'

'I'm sorry about that,' Gilby said

sarcastically. 'But Stirzaker's been running some crooked games, and I figure I need some help keeping this town in line. Once word gets out that people like Stirzaker can get away with rigging their games, anything can happen.'

'I guess you're right,' Forrester shrugged. 'We'll just have to hope you can keep the lid on things.'

Gilby gave him a sour look. That night Gilby did his rounds. When he came to the alley out of which Roy Carson and Mercy had come, he felt sick. A cat came running out of the alley. Gilby drew his gun, and found his hand shaking.

'Near thing, Sheriff,' a voice called out from somewhere up the street.

Gilby squinted into the dark, but could see nothing. A few seconds later, he heard someone laughing, and figured it might be Stirzaker, or one of his boys. He ran up the street towards the noise, but could see nothing. A cold sweat had broken out on his forehead. With the back of his hand he wiped it away. The street was empty. All he could hear was the noise from the Fair Lady.

The sheriff pushed in through the batwing doors and looked round.

Straightaway, the noise from the tinkling piano died away. The player on the stool turned round. At the bar, everybody put their drinks down and turned to look at him. Suddenly Gilby felt pretty stupid. Stirzaker came out of the back, like he had been expecting him.

'Drink, Sheriff? You look as though you could use one. Barney,' he called out.

'Yeah, boss,' the barkeep said.

'Drink for the sheriff.' Stirzaker lit his cigar, and blew out a puff of dark-blue smoke. His eyes followed it up to the ceiling.

Barney took down a glass and filled it. He put it on the bar.

'Keep it,' Gilby said, and walked out of the saloon.

As he went through the doors he

heard them laughing. The night air was cool and it cleared his mind as he continued on his rounds and returned to his office. He went out at midnight to do his final check. The Fair Lady was on the point of closing as he went past. As he got to the edge of the boardwalk, he heard more laughing behind him. Something in him snapped. He walked back to the crowd.

'Everything all right?' he asked them.

'Sure, everything's all right, with us,' one of them said. 'How about you, Sheriff? You don't look so good.'

Gilby bit his lip, and headed back to his office. From the desk he took the whiskey bottle and poured a stiff measure into his mug. Putting the cork back in, he made up his mind. That night, Gilby slept alone in his own bed, with a feeling of warmth from the whiskey.

The next morning, Gilby went down to his office, where he found Forrester waiting for him. He took off his star and tossed it on the desk.

'I think you'd better find another sheriff,' he told the mayor.

'Sorry it has to end like this,' Forrester said, picking up the star and looking at Gilby. 'But I think it's for the best.'

'So do I,' Gilby agreed.

4

Frank Gilby hauled off the trail and guided his horse down between the low hanging branches of the trees that would provide him with a degree of protection from the heat of the day. It had been a couple of months since he had shot Roy Carson, and he and his wife had gone their separate ways, but he still felt numb inside.

Gilby had been riding all morning and figured that the time had come to give his horse and himself a break, and eat the sandwiches that the girl in the café had fixed for him before he had ridden out of the town where he had been working as a security guard for a bank. Sliding out of the saddle, he caught hold of the leathers of his horse and fastened them round a tree. He stretched his aching body and eased his back after the long ride. Taking down the canteen, he put it to his lips and took a long drink, then he poured some into his hands and gave it to his horse.

Sitting down, he opened the packet of sandwiches and began to eat them. They sure tasted good, he thought, as he lay beneath the tree enjoying the sun. When he had eaten enough, he rolled himself a stogie and put a match to it. He watched the smoke curl up among the branches of the trees. Life was sure good after the last couple of months, he thought.

'Makin' yerself damn comfortable?' The voice was as loud and ornery as it was unexpected.

Gilby jumped to his feet, his hand dropping to the butt of his gun.

'Keep still, or you'll be collectin' a bullet,' the same ornery voice said. 'Like you've been handing out to God-fearing ranchers hereabouts.'

Gilby froze his hand hovering over the gun. His body was stiff and tense, waiting for the bullet.

'Delilah, get his .45, and watch the rustlin' sidewinder,' the voice went on.

'Sure, Pa.' Gilby heard a girl's voice answer from somewhere behind him.

From the corner of his eye, he saw a good-looking black-haired girl reaching down to his holster to relieve him of his gun. When she had lifted it out of the leather, he heard her step back.

'Now, let's see what you look like from the front,' a fresh voice said.

Slowly, his hands still raised, Gilby turned.

There were three of them, all members of the same family, he reckoned. The ornery-voiced old man was holding an old Winchester, a younger man, his son, dressed the same as his pa, an evil, sadistic look on his thin face. Beside him stood his sister, a girl with long black hair that shone in the sunlight. Her face was pretty and had a mischievous grin on it.

'We finally got one of them,' the old man said.

'Yeah.' The smile on the girl's face widened. 'And a right handsome one, he is too.'

'Damn it, Delilah,' cursed the old man in a furious voice. 'You sound like yer ma used to sound, an' a right low-speaking woman she was.'

'Hell, Pa,' the girl went on. 'I'm just sayin' he's right handsome, which anybody can see.'

'Hush yer mouth, girl,' the old man said.

'Yeah, we ain't got all day, if we're gonna string this rustler up,' the young man next to her said.

'What do you mean rustler?' Gilby hollered, involuntarily taking a step forward.

The old man tightened his finger on the trigger. Dust kicked up just in front of Gilby's foot.

'Stay where you are,' the old man told him, once the sound of the shot had died away.

Gilby froze, the hatred was etched in the old man's face, like he was just waiting for Gilby to do something stupid.

'I'm no rustler,' he tried again. 'I used to be a lawman.'

'Like hell you used to be a lawman,' the old man said. 'Like I'm the Archangel Gabriel.'

The younger man stepped forward and made to strike Gilby, but the girl caught his hand and held it. From what Gilby could see she had a fearsome grip. The younger man winced before shrugging, and pulling his hand away.

'What are you going to do?' Gilby asked the old man.

'We're gonna string you up,' he said.

Gilby looked from one to the other. Their eyes were full of venom and hatred for him.

'You crazy old bastard,' he stormed at them. 'You can't go round hanging anybody you feel like. That's murder.'

'We've got a gun and a rope,' the old man said. 'And they say we can.'

'Save yer breath for when you're hanging,' the younger man said.

There was a tone of finality in his voice, that made Gilby go cold.

'I've got an idea,' the younger man added.

'What's that, Matthew?' the old man asked him.

There was a sudden interest in the old man's voice that Gilby knew boded no good for him.

'If we're gonna hang this critter, maybe we should brand him, and let the Lord recognize him for what he is.'

'Sounds like a good idea to me,' the old man agreed.

Gilby watched as the face of the girl turned deathly pale. She looked at her pa.

'You can't let Matthew do that. It ain't right,' she gasped, putting her hand to her mouth, and biting the knuckle hard.

'Right or not,' the old man said, 'I'm gonna do it. Fellas like this are goin' to be the ruination of us all.'

'I'll get the fire started. I've got an old branding-iron in my saddle-bag,'

Matthew said sadistically.

Gilby felt sick at the thought. He glanced from the old man to the girl as Matthew went to get the branding-iron, weighing up the chances of jumping them, and maybe grabbing a gun.

'I can see what yer thinkin',' the old man said suddenly. 'Delilah, go get a rope so we can tie this rustlin' crittur up,' he snarled, poking the air with the Winchester.

Reluctantly, the girl went to get a rope. When she came back, the old man snatched it from her and thrust the gun into her hands.

'Keep him covered while I tie him up,' the old man said to her. 'She's as good a shot as me,' he said to Gilby.

He walked behind Gilby and pulled Gilby's hands down behind his back. Roughly he tied them together, then hauled him to a tree where he fastened him to it.

Matthew came back into the clearing, holding the branding-iron.

'I'll get a fire goin', pa,' he said,

gathering up some dried wood and heaping it between a ring of stones, then he took a box of Vestas from his pocket and got the fire going. When it was going strong, he put the iron into it and let it get red hot.

The sweat broke out on Gilby's forehead. It ran down through the trail dust on his face. He felt his arms shaking. The old man came across to him. Savagely, he ripped open Gilby's shirt.

'I told you he was a handsome fella,' the girl said, her voice a mixture of fear and admiration.

'It's about ready, Pa,' Matthew called out.

He had taken a rag from his pocket and had folded it round the handle of the branding-iron. Picking it up, he walked slowly across to Gilby, the air in front of the iron, shimmering. Matthew walked slowly enjoying every moment of it, as he watched Gilby's strained face with beads of sweat breaking out on it.

The girl had gone to sit on a tree-trunk and was chewing on a stalk of grass, her face pale and sick-looking.

The ropes bit into Gilby's wrists as Matthew came for him, the branding-iron getting bigger and redder in front of him. As hard as he strained he could not get free of the ropes holding him to the tree. Matthew raised the brand and drove it into Gilby's flesh.

Gilby heard himself scream as he fell into the black hole that was waiting for him. The pain scorched through his body, again and again, and when he opened his eyes it was still there, along with the smell of his burning hide and Matthew's sadistic face.

'It's OK, Pa, he's still alive,' he heard the voice of the young man say, gleefully.

'Damn you, Matthew, there weren't no need for that.' That was the girl shouting, the black-haired girl with green eyes whom the old man called Delilah.

'Hush yer mouth, girl,' the old man

said to her, his voice shaking with fury.

'But, Pa, that's damn wrong what you let Matthew do to this fella,' she went on, her voice still shaking.

Gilby could visualize her sitting on the tree stump chewing on the stalk of grass, just before her brother Matthew had stuck the red-hot branding-iron into him.

'I told you to quit it,' the old man went on.

'But Pa,' she said again.

Then Gilby heard the sound of the slap and the girl cried out in pain. He tried to wrench his head round to see what was happening, but the old man had done his job well when he had tied him to the tree. The girl cried out again as her pa's open hand landed on the side of her face.

'Damn you, Delilah, like I said, you've got yer ma's sinful ways,' the old man snarled at her.

'We gonna string him up, Pa?' Matthew asked him, striding round from behind the tree so that Gilby could see him.

Matthew had his pa's thin face, and ferret-like eyes. The old man wore a long black coat and had a Bible sticking out of the pocket. He stood sneering at Gilby, his hands on his hips, a sadistic gleam in his eyes, like he was really enjoying it.

Delilah was sobbing softly as the old man joined Matthew.

'Git his rope an' fashion a noose,' the old man said.

Matthew turned and walked to where Gilby's horse was tethered. Through narrowed eyes, Gilby watched as he took his rope from his saddle horn and twisted one end into a noose. The rope snaked up into the air and fell across a branch. Matthew pulled it down and tied the free end to the tree, and brought Gilby's horse over to where Gilby could see it.

The pain in Gilby's hide was still burning like one of the fires of Hell. Matthew, helped by his pa, untied him from the tree, and dragged him up into the saddle, pulling the noose round his neck. Gilby fought hard, but the two of them were too much and the branding had taken a lot of his strength out of him.

'You ready, boy?' the old man asked.

'Sure am, Pa.' Matthew answered, getting ready to slap the horse from under Gilby.

'We'd better let his Maker know he's on his way up,' the old man said, pulling the dog-eared Bible from his coat pocket.

'You got a name?' he asked Gilby.

'Yeah, but it isn't for the likes of you,' Gilby gasped, his vision swimming with the pain.

The old man glared up at him, then licked a thin finger and flicked through the pages, until he found what he was looking for. Taking off his hat, he indicated for Matthew and the girl to kneel down, then started to recite 'The Lord is my Shepherd.'

When he had finished he stood up.

'You got anything to say?' he shouted up to Gilby.

Through the pain, Gilby looked down at him.

'This is murder, you miserable old man,' he swore through the pain.

'What you an' yer boys have bin doin' to the spreads round here is pretty well the same thing,' the old man said, putting the Bible back into his pocket.

'Damn you, old man,' Gilby shouted, the rope biting into his neck, the pain in his flesh getting worse.

'You ready, Pa?' Matthew asked his father, as he raised his hand to strike the horse's rump.

5

'No, he ain't ready,' Gilby heard a woman's voice say from behind him. 'Dennis, you steady that fella's horse. I don't want him hanging by accident.'

Gilby's horse skittered, as one of the riders approached and held it.

'Now, a couple of you boys help cut him down,' the woman went on.

A knife sliced through the rope around Gilby's neck, another knife sliced through the rope holding his hands. The pain was less now. Gilby tried to croak his thanks, but the words stuck in his throat.

'Just take it easy, fella,' a friendly voice said at his side. 'Get him down, and get a bandage for this burn.'

Gently Gilby was lowered from the saddle and laid on the ground.

'Just what's yer game, Helena Good-night?' he heard the preacher-like voice of the old man call out.

'My game's catching the real rustlers, and stopping you hanging innocent men,' Helena called back, her voice hard and angry.

'So how come you know he's innocent?' Delilah snapped at Helena, getting up from the stump.

Gilby had been raised to a sitting position, a rough bandage around his body. Delilah was standing in front of the woman, her hands on her hips, a defiant attitude to her stance.

'How do you know he's guilty, Delilah?' Helena Goodnight started to get down from her horse. She stood in front of Delilah, matching her in stance, and looking her in the eye.

Delilah seemed to crumble as Helena held her gaze.

'Damn it, he looks guilty,' Matthew yelled, coming to stand by his sister.

'You're a fine one to talk,' Helena said, pointing to Matthew. 'Just take a good long look at what you've done.'

'We caught him,' Matthew yelled angrily.

'Doing what, exactly?' she demanded.

Matthew could not answer this. He stood looking like he wanted to throw a punch at Helena, but one of the men with her stepped between them giving Matthew a push that sent him sprawling into the dust.

'Isaiah Parker,' Helena said to him. 'You and your brood saddle up and get off Flying G land,' she said.

'May the good Lord forgive you,' Isaiah said loudly, waving his fist in her face.

'You're a Bible-spouting hypocrite,' Helena said to him. 'Now, like I said, get out of here so we can get this fella fixed up proper.'

Isaiah and the others walked to their horses, their gait displaying their anger.

'You feeling any better now?' Helena Goodnight asked Gilby as she came to kneel down beside him.

'Yeah, I'm feeling a heap better now you got that noose from round my neck,' Gilby managed to tell her, his voice still croaking.

'Glad to hear it,' she said. 'You get him up on his horse, and be careful, that crittur Matthew's branded him. He said he would if he caught one of them damned rustlers.'

'Yeah, he's the sort who would,' Dennis Morgan said, putting his hand under Gilby's arm and easing him to his feet. 'Can you walk all right?'

'I figure so,' Gilby said, with a groan. With the help of two of the ranch hands Gilby was taken to his horse and helped into the saddle. With every movement came a fresh flooding of the fire along his side. When they were mounted they rode out of the clearing, Dennis Morgan riding up close to him to stop him falling out of the saddle.

As they topped a rise, Gilby became aware of the ranch house below them. It looked a prosperous place, and well set up. As they rode into the yard, the door of the house opened.

'Hi, Sam,' Helena called out. 'Send

one of the hands into town to get Doc
Bannister and get him back here. This
fella's hurt.'

'OK, boss,' Sam called back.

They half carried Gilby into the
house and up the stairs to a room at
the back.

He could feel them getting his
clothes off him, and putting him into
the bed. Then the light faded and he
could feel himself struggling on a sea of
fire.

He kicked and twisted against the
sheets, seeing Matthew's devilish, grinning face, the iron in his hands. He
heard Delilah scream.

'Doc's here,' the cook said.

The doc was tubby and well dressed,
with a small black bag under his arm.
He had a jovial face

'Helena told me what happened.
That damn Matthew.' He put the bag
down on the table, and pulled back the
sheets. Taking a pair of scissors from his
bag the doc cut through the bandages.

'Yeah, it's going to take some time to

heal,' he said in an Eastern accent. 'I'll put something on to keep the infection down, and give you something to make sure you get a good night's sleep.' It took him ten minutes to apply some soothing ointment and a clean bandage. Straightaway, Gilby started to feel a lessening of the pain.

'Thanks, Doc,' Gilby said, shifting in the bed.

'I'll come back in a day or so,' Doc Bannister said, picking up his bag and going for the door.

Gilby lay back in the pillows and put his hands to his eyes, trying to blot out the image of Roy Carson, the banker's son, dying in the trough. There had been a time when he thought he was over it and the nightmares had gone away. Now it seemed it was coming back to haunt him again, and the nightmare of Mercy going down to the Wells Fargo office. Once or twice he caught himself wondering what had happened to her.

He twisted over on his side and

immediately regretted it as the pain hit him again. He groaned and twisted on to his back.

'Heard you groaning while I was outside,' the cook said, as he came into the room.

Gilby wiped a thin line of sweat out of his eyes.

'The doc's left you something for the pain,' the cook said.

Gilby tried to sit up.

'Just stay where you are, I'll bring it up.' The cook put a hand on his chest to hold him in the bed. 'I'll get you something to eat.'

He came back ten minutes later, with a tray.

'Best Flying G beefsteak with potatoes and gravy,' he said cheerfully, putting the tray down on the table beside the bed.

Stretching out, he helped Gilby to sit up.

'Want a hand with the eating irons?' he asked, taking them up from the tray.

'Guess not,' Gilby told him. 'Just cut

up that steak for me and I can do the rest.'

Sam laughed. 'I'll be back later. The doc left something to make sure you git a good night's sleep.'

When he had gone Gilby's appetite suddenly returned. Soon he had the plate cleared, and the coffee drunk.

'Figured you'd be finished by now,' Sam said, when he came back.

He handed Gilby a glass. 'This is what the doc left,' he grinned. 'You'd best be drinking it.'

'Thanks,' Gilby said, with a sour face.

'Probably tastes like that, too.' Sam picked up the tray and left Gilby to get some sleep.

It was dark when Gilby opened his eyes. Something, he didn't know what, had woken him. He moved restlessly, his side still burning. The noise came again. A soft footfall outside the room. Instinctively Gilby reached for his gun. His hand clawed at the empty air as the pain made him wince. Beads of sweat broke out on his forehead. His gun was in the holster, slung over the chair across the room. He vaguely remembered one of the ranch hands picking it up in the clearing.

The door of the next room opened and he heard voices. Helena was talking quietly. The other voice he seemed to recognize, but couldn't. He thought that it might be that of her husband. Gilby rolled on to his left side and tried to sleep, as the sounds of lovemaking came from the room. Gilby squirmed with embarrassment, as the noises became more feverish and hectic. The lovemaking seemed to go on for a long time, but in the end it finished, and Gilby relaxed. He sat up, his head against the board at his back. The voices came again. Helena's, and the other man. For a second, he heard the other voice clearly: it was Dennis Morgan, the foreman of the ranch.

The realization jerked Gilby fully awake. Dennis Morgan and Helena. Then he told himself that it was none of his business; still, it made him feel uncomfortable. For a spell there was silence, then the door of the room opened and he heard footsteps going quietly down the corridor. His curiosity got the better of him. Easing himself out of the bed, he padded across to the window.

Dennis Morgan was crossing the yard to the bunkhouse; as he got there, he veered away and went into the stable. Intrigued, Gilby remained where he was. A few minutes later, Dennis Morgan emerged, leading his horse. He walked to the gate of the ranch entrance, mounted and rode off into the night.

6

Dennis Morgan rode away from the Flying G feeling satisfied with himself. Everything was going fine with Helena, and tonight they'd make another killing when they hit the herd of the Broken Spur.

He rode on to where the trail split to Centreville and headed off to the Broken Spur land. Ahead of him he saw four riders silhouetted against the moon.

'That you, Dennis?' Brad Colville shouted to him.

'Yeah, it's me, Brad,' Morgan replied, pulling on the leathers of his horse. 'The old Bible-basher's watering his beeves down by the creek where his land comes on to Flying G's.'

'He got any new men?' Colville asked him, sliding his Winchester out of the saddle holster.

'No, he's too mean to lay out any dough fer any extra help,' Morgan said.

'Let's git then,' Colville said, heading towards the creek.

* * *

Isaiah was singing a psalm to the bedded-down beeves. Matthew was somewhere just the other side of the herd. His sister was in the shelter of a stand of trees, fixing up some coffee for him and his pa. The night had a habit of turning cold after the heat of the day. It was looking like rain was coming in as well. If it did, she decided, it would be one hell of a storm.

She pulled the blanket around her and cursed the rustlers. For a moment, she thought of Frank Gilby and was glad they hadn't strung him up. He was a right handsome fella, and there weren't too many of them around. Helena's boy Michael was turning out handsome, but at the moment that was all he was, a boy. Frank Gilby was something different. A real man. You could see that in the way he handled himself when they had the rope around his neck.

She poured the thick black coffee into the two mugs, and stood up and stretched. The cold night air had made her buxom body cold and stiff, despite the blanket. After she had stretched she headed to the horses. She led her own back to the camp-fire. Taking one mug, she rode out to where her pa was, meaning to come back for Matthew's.

A peal of thunder came across the sky just as the first rifle shot rang out. The sound startled her and she tipped the coffee to the ground. Behind her, she could see the horsemen coming her way, the flashes from their guns coming hard and fast through the lashing rain. To her surprise, they ignored her, and rode past. Grabbing the stock of her old Winchester, she went after them.

Didn't they know they were driving her family out of business and had to be stopped? Isaiah and Matthew heard the shooting and headed in its direction. The two groups collided head on. Isaiah wheeled and fired as Colville went by him. The bullet took off Colville's hat and grazed his skull.

Colville swore and rode on in the direction of the herd. 'Start cutting some of them beeves out,' he yelled at Davies. 'Get them out to the valley.'

'OK, boss,' came the answer from Davies.

Colville turned his horse and went back in the direction of Matthew, as angry as hell at nearly collecting some lead in his skull. He levered another shell into the breech. Out ahead of him, he saw the darkened figure of Matthew hurtling down on him, his rifle to his shoulder.

Matthew had seen the figure coming his way. Like Colville, his anger was in control. Levelling his rifle at Colville, he sent a round his way. The bullet missed. Bringing up his own rifle to his shoulder, he threw a hunk of lead back at Matthew.

The bullet missed Matthew's head because of the bumpy ground, but hit the mare in the forehead. The animal bucked and fell. Matthew fell with her, but managed to roll clear of the flailing hooves of Colville's charging horse. As he rode past, Colville knew that he had missed and fired another shot as Matthew struggled to his feet.

Matthew was lucky again as the lead passed close to his head. Colville was bearing down on him once more as Delilah saw them. She fired without aiming, trusting to luck. The bullet was close enough to spoil Colville's aim.

Hauling on the leathers of his horse, Colville bore away to find the rest of the gang who were driving off the herd. Delilah swore as Colville wheeled away. She pushed the Winchester into her saddle holster and bent low in the saddle extending her hand to her brother.

'Come on, Matt, we got to see if Pa's OK,' she said, as Matthew grabbed her hand and swung himself up behind her.

'I ain't one of yer admirers,' he said, 'but that was a slick piece of shooting.'

'Yeah,' the girl grunted, as she rowelled her horse in the direction of where her pa was supposed to be.

They pounded on through the night, the clouds low and heavy with the rain. As they reached the edge of the creek, a fork of lightning split the sky and the water came down as though the heavens had torn apart. The rain pounded their bodies as they searched for Isaiah. Another fork of lightning lit up the scene.

'There he is,' Delilah called out, pointing to him as he emerged from a stand of trees.

As he got into the clearing, a bolt of lightning hit the tallest of the trees, splitting it from top to bottom. The two halves hit the ground just behind Isaiah, who didn't even turn round.

'That was close, Pa,' Delilah said, concern in her voice.

'The Lord had His hand on me,' Isaiah said, in a sanctimonious voice over another roll of thunder.

Neither of the others spoke. Instead, they just looked round in the growing storm.

'Now we ain't gonna find those beeves tonight,' Isaiah shouted above the noise.

'We're gonna have to try,' Matthew shouted back. 'This herd's getting smaller and smaller every time they hit us. Pretty soon we ain't gonna have a herd left.'

The old man scowled. 'I guess we'd better start lookin'.'

They rode off into the teeth of the storm.

★ ★ ★

Sam woke Gilby pretty early. The rain had not long stopped and the place looked fresh after the long spell of hot weather.

'Food on the table if you've a mind,' he said, after he had shaken Gilby awake.

Gilby pushed himself up against the pillows, his mind taking a minute to clear.

'I'm feeling pretty hungry after that storm,' he said.

'Yeah, it was a bad one,' Sam replied, opening the door. 'Just come down when you're ready.'

Gilby got out of bed. His body still ached from the branding, but it had steadied down a mite. Fresh water and a towel and shaving gear stood by the bowl. Taking his time, he washed up and had a sort of shave. Then he went downstairs. On his way down, he could hear Helena and Sam talking. Straight-away he remembered what he had heard the previous night. He wondered if Helena would have known he was in the next room.

When he saw her he realized that she knew that he might have heard her and Dennis Morgan.

'Care for some breakfast, Frank?' she asked him, as he came to the table.

'Sure,' he said, thinking how strained she looked.

'Sam,' she called out to the kitchen, 'bring another plate in for Frank.'

The cook came in holding a plate piled high with grub. He put it down in front of Gilby and went to pour some coffee for him.

'Bad storm last night,' Helena said after awhile.

'Yes, it kept me awake,' Gilby said.

He realized that he had said the wrong thing.

Helena's face flushed up as he spoke. They were silent as Sam poured the coffee. Gilby ate in silence until he heard a horse galloping into the yard.

'Dennis's back,' Helena said, seeing him looking out of the window. 'He's been up all night. We've been having some trouble with rustlers.'

'I know,' Gilby replied, wondering just where Dennis Morgan had been all night.

They continued to eat, then Gilby heard a wagon coming into the yard.

Again, Helena looked flushed and worried. The wagon stopped and Gilby heard the creak of the harness and the snorting of horses. This time Helena said nothing.

A few minutes later, he heard the rumbling of wheels on the veranda outside, then the door opened. He looked round as Dennis Morgan pushed a wheelchair into the house. The occupant was a sour-looking man, with what had once been a powerful build. Helena stood up and gave Gilby a worried look.

'This is my husband, Richard,' she said, as her husband wheeled himself into the dining-room. 'Richard, this is Frank Gilby.'

The man in the chair looked Gilby up and down. Gilby thought that if he looked like that at some men Gilby had known, he would have got a beating. Richard Goodnight dismissed Gilby with a look. Gilby had stood up, his hand outstretched, but it was ignored.

Helena looked at her husband.

'Frank's looking for work. I thought perhaps we had something.'

'Sam,' Richard Goodnight bawled suddenly.

The door opened and Sam came in with another plate in his hand. Richard Goodnight wheeled himself to a chairless place at the head of the table, but did not speak.

Gilby watched him dig into his food. He ate quickly and with a fair amount of relish. Soon the plate was empty. He rapped on the table with his fork and Sam came in with another plate. He attacked the second plate with the same relish and soon had that cleared. As he pushed it to one side, Dennis Morgan came into the house.

'Trouble, Captain,' Morgan said, jerking his thumb over his shoulder at the door.

'What kind of trouble, Dennis?' Goodnight asked him.

'It's that old fool Isaiah,' Morgan told Goodnight.

'Well, we'd better go and see what

this old fool wants.' There was something in his tone that made Gilby look up.

He slammed his napkin down on the table, grabbed the rims of his wheelchair and swung himself clear of the table.

Morgan followed his boss out of the house and on to the veranda, Gilby and Helena went with them.

Isaiah was on his horse flanked by a weary-looking Delilah and Matthew.

He also looked tired and worried.

'There he is,' Isaiah exclaimed, when he saw Gilby standing in front of Helena.

'Yes,' Helena retorted angrily, 'and if it hadn't been for us we would have been cutting him down this morning.'

The captain started forward in his chair, and swung his powerful neck round in Helena's direction. 'Stay out of this Helena.'

Gilby felt Helena flinch at the sharp words from her husband.

'Yes, Richard,' she said angrily,

glancing down at her husband.

Isaiah looked thunderously in Gilby's direction. 'That fella's friends hit my herd again last night. Near killed Delilah and Matthew.'

'Neither would be a great loss,' Helena snapped.

The captain tried to swing round again, but she was too far behind him.

'Helena, go into the house,' he snapped at her.

Gilby thought that if the look could have killed, the captain wouldn't have needed his chair any more. White-faced, Helena turned from the veranda and walked into the house. He caught the look on the foreman's face.

'Now, what's this about, Isaiah?' the captain said, with some sympathy in his voice.

'Like I said,' Isaiah went on, pointing at Gilby, 'this fella's friends hit my herd last night.'

'He wasn't anywhere near your herd last night,' the captain said. 'Thanks to you, Matthew, he spent the night here.

Like you, I'm a rancher, Isaiah, so I can feel some sympathy for you, but until you've learned some manners, get off my land and stay off.'

'I'm goin', Captain, but this ain't the end of it, an' if me or Matthew find him off this spread, we're gonna do a proper job of lynchin' him.'

The three of them rode out of the ranch yard. Delilah gave a look over her shoulder to Gilby as they went through the gate.

Richard Goodnight swung his chair round and, followed by Morgan, went back inside. His wife was at the table, white-faced and picking at the remains of her breakfast. She looked up at him as he came in, the same hateful look in her eyes.

'Do you have to speak to me like that in front of other people, Richard?' she said.

The captain wheeled himself back to his position at the head of the table.

'I do when you take it on yourself to interfere with the running of the ranch,' he snapped at her.

Helena slammed down her cutlery and made to go for the stairs; as she did so a young man came downstairs. He looked bleary-eyed and untidy.

'G'morning,' he said shakily, like he was still drunk.

'Good morning, my boy,' the captain said in the most civil tone that Gilby had heard him use.

'You're still drunk.' Helena's voice was full of disgust.

'Just tied a few on last night. Jimmy Higgins is goin' back East to study. Won't be seeing him for awhile.' He collapsed into a chair.

'Have you been seeing that no-good tramp Delilah?' Helena asked angrily.

'Not last night, I didn't,' he replied, moving back out of the way as Sam came in with a cup of coffee for him.

'So if he has been seeing Delilah, what about it? She's the kind of girl every boy should see before they settle down,' the captain interposed. 'I did it before I married you; I dare say your brother did it too. It prepares a man for married life,' Richard Goodnight said coarsely.

'There are times when you disgust me, Richard,' Helena said, flouncing up the stairs.

'I guess I'll be going,' Gilby said, finishing his cold coffee.

'I've given it some thought, but I'm sorry I can't oblige you with a job,' Richard Goodnight said, without looking up.

As he walked over to the stable, Gilby wondered if Dennis Morgan had anything to do with the rustling. He sure wasn't taking the night air for the sake of his health after sporting with his boss's wife. Putting the thought out of his mind, he went into the barn.

'You got my horse ready?' he asked the fella in the stable when he got in there.

'Yeah, fed, watered and rested,' the man said, putting his broom against the end of the wall.

'You have any trouble with her?'

Gilby asked him, as he put on the leathers.

'Hell, no,' he was told. 'Quiet as a lamb.' The man grinned, giving the horse's neck a friendly pat.

'That's a sight more than can be said about them up there,' Gilby said, indicating the house, and encouraging the man to talk.

The man took the bait.

'Them two, I don't know why they stay together,' he said, looking down the aisle of the stable. 'The captain used to be a pretty regular fella, then the war came and changed it all.'

'War can do things like that,' Gilby said, taking the leathers off the man.

'It wasn't just that. He collected a bullet in the spine when some prisoners broke out of the prison camp where he was stationed. Been in a chair ever since.'

'He still seems like a tough old bird,' Gilby said.

'You can say that again,' the stable hand said, as Gilby rode out.

7

Centreville was beginning to grow. The railroad had come through a year back; more people had come with it to settle, and open more shops and stores. Gilby noticed all this as he rode in. He even noticed the vacancy sign for a sheriff, and wondered about it, but he wasn't going to apply for it, not after last time. There was a big new store with the name 'Tolliver's Emporium' painted bright and fresh over it. He noticed the woman standing outside with a brush in her hands, and the way she looked at him.

It had been a while since he had eaten and his hunger was starting to make itself felt. Keeping his eyes open for a café, he saw one on the end of the block that looked pretty reasonable.

Sliding out of the saddle, he hitched the horse to the rail and went in. The place seemed warm and friendly, and he could smell the food cooking in the back. Gilby hung his hat on the hook and sat down.

'I thought I heard somebody coming in,' a friendly-looking cook said, when he had come through the curtain.

'I just got into town, and need something to eat,' Gilby told him.

'You sure you got the money to eat here?' the cook asked.

Gilby rummaged in his pockets and took out what was the last of his money. He spread it out on the table.

'You've got about enough,' the cook told him. 'I can't give you much, but I can give you something,' he said with a smile.

'Thanks,' Gilby said, wiping his hands on his trousers.

'Just sit there, it won't be long.' The cook disappeared.

Gilby sat looking at the table, waiting for the cook to come back.

'From the look of you, things have been pretty tough,' the cook said, when he had laid the stuff out on the table.

'You could say that,' Gilby answered, picking up his fork.

'From the looks of that scar on yer neck it could have been a lot tougher.' The cook had sat down and was giving him some pretty curious looks.

Gilby told him about what had happened, as he cut up his food and started to eat. The cook watched him in silence, nodding occasionally.

'Yeah, I can see their thinking. The rustlers have been having it their own way for a spell now.'

'I kinda figured that,' Gilby replied.

'You might have noticed we've got a vacancy for a sheriff.' The cook shifted in his chair. 'My name's Al Starret, by the way.' He reached over and took Gilby's hand.

'Frank Gilby,' came the answer.

'Where were you sheriff of?' Starret asked him.

Gilby looked up sharply, a look of surprise on his face.

'How'd you know I was a lawman?'

he asked quickly.

'Just a guess, and the two holes in yer shirt where the badge used to go,' Starret said with a grin.

'You're pretty observant for a cook,' Gilby told him, wiping his mouth with the napkin.

'I'm not only a cook, I'm the mayor as well, and I've done time, but that was a long time back. It's all behind me now.'

'OK, I believe you,' Gilby told him.

'So how come you ain't a sheriff now?' Starret asked him.

Gilby thought about it, then told Starret.

'I can see how that would happen on a dark street,' Starret said.

Gilby was surprised at the sympathy in his voice.

'It sounds like you're offering me the job,' he said.

'Yeah, I've got to offer it to somebody. You've had the experience. You've got to put what happened at the back of you. Like I said, I can understand how it could happen on a dark street even after you shouted a warning.'

As he thought about it, he fingered the scar on his neck. If Helena Goodnight and her boys hadn't come along, he might still be out there with the rope round his neck and his tongue hanging out. Then there was the Parker clan. Maybe he owed them something. He sure as hell didn't like the idea of them riding round the range handing out their own kind of justice to the wrong people. They were in enough trouble.

'So you're going to take the job, are you?' he heard Starret ask him.

'I'm going to take it, even if it's just to show Parker that he's wrong.'

Starret grinned, and held out his hand again.

'Glad you said that. I was beginning to think I had you figured wrong.'

Starret got up. 'I'm going to lock up. I'll see you down at the sheriff's office, after I've gone and got the keys. You know where it is: you passed it on your way into town.'

'Yeah. See you down there,' Gilby said, pushing back the chair and getting up.

He followed Starret out into the street. Then headed down towards the office while Starret went to get the keys. When he passed Tolliver's Emporium, he noticed the same woman watching him as he went past.

Starret caught up with him at the office just after he got there. When he unlocked the door and opened it, Gilby knew the place hadn't been occupied for a spell.

'I'll open some of the windows,' Starret said, as he went round pulling at the catches. 'And I think I'll see if I can get somebody to clean the place up.'

After he had finished, Starret opened a desk drawer and took out a dusty star.

'Raise yer right hand,' he instructed Gilby, and then swore him in.

Gilby felt a heap better when the star was back on his chest.

'Take a turn round the town. Let people get used to your face and the star on your vest,' Starret instructed him.

★ ★ ★

Dennis Morgan met Brad Colville in the valley just on the Flying G land. Colville looked pretty pleased with himself.

'We got thirty head last night,' Colville said to Morgan.

'Glad to hear it,' Morgan said, when he had taken his cut of the last raid on Flying G beeves and stuffed it into his vest pocket.

'I ain't too pleased,' Colville said. 'This neck of the woods is getting played out. Maybe it's time we were looking for somewhere fresh.'

For a moment Morgan considered what his boss had said. 'Yeah, I think maybe yer right.'

Colville leaned across his saddle. 'Say, you remember me scouting this

85

land a while back before we got fixed up together?'

'Yeah, sure I remember,' Morgan said, digging the makings out of his vest and starting to build a stogie.

'That woman you were sporting with down in that stand of trees; who was she? You remember, a Saturday, I think it was.'

Morgan looked at him. 'You spyin' on me?' he said with a laugh.

'Hell, no. I don't need that kinda thing. I reckon I know her. What's her name?'

'Her name?' Morgan asked in surprise.

'Yeah, her name.' Colville built himself a stogie and put a match to it.

'Helena Goodnight,' Morgan said, as he lit his own cigarette.

Colville's reaction took him by surprise.

'Wife of Captain Richard Goodnight?' Colville asked, when he had finished laughing.

'Yeah. The same fella. He's in a chair.

Got a Reb bullet in his back in the war,' Morgan said uneasily.

'Yeah, and I know who put it there,' Colville said.

'Who? Anybody I know?' Morgan asked, with a laugh.

'Me, you dummy,' Colville said, then hawked and spat into the dust.

'You nearly did for old iron breeches Goodnight?'

'Yeah, I sure did. And that sweet little wife of his supplied me with the gun,' Colville went on, shaking with laughter.

Morgan looked up at the sky, and laughed again.

'I gotta get back. He's bringing in some new riding horses for me to look at, and I've got to be back at the ranch for one o'clock. You can tell me some more some other time.'

'I'll do that,' Colville promised him.

The men separated and went their different ways.

8

Gilby was taking Starret's advice, and showing himself round the town.

As Colville and Morgan were splitting up, Frank Gilby was doing a tour of the red light part of town, taking in all the faces, whom he knew from experience were the ones who would give him trouble. Then he walked down the saloon fronts, then into the part of town where the shops and stores were.

He stopped outside Tolliver's Emporium, and looked in through the window. The woman, whom Starret had told him was Elizabeth Tolliver, was standing by the counter showing a bolt of cloth to a customer. She glanced up from the counter and looked at Gilby. Seeing him watching her, she signalled him to come in. Gilby went inside as the customer, an attractive woman in her early thirties, turned to look at what

Elizabeth Tolliver was doing.

'I'm glad to see we've got a new sheriff,' she said, to a man coming in through the curtain from the back. 'I'm Elizabeth Tolliver and this is my husband Jack.'

'Pleased to meet you. I'm Frank Gilby,' he replied, touching his hat.

'And I'm Kathy Travers,' the customer said.

Gilby looked at her. He could see that she was prettier than she looked from the outside.

'We're sure glad we've got a new sheriff,' Jack Tolliver said, holding out his hand.

It felt soft and fleshy and cold to Gilby. Tolliver had a weak chin. Not too much spine, Gilby thought. Elizabeth Tolliver, he reckoned, wore the pants in the house, or maybe the store. Kathy Travers was something else again, he thought.

'Yes, we can feel safer now that we have a real man in town,' Elizabeth Tolliver smiled up at him.

A real man-eater, Gilby told himself, as he tried to shake off her hand that had somehow wound its way around his. Definitely to be handled with kid gloves, he told himself.

'I've got to be going, Elizabeth,' Kathy said, giving Gilby a quick look.

'Fine, Kathy,' Elizabeth Tolliver said, as Kathy went out into the street.

Gilby saw a strange look cross Jack Tolliver's face, like he wanted to say something, but hadn't got the nerve.

'You going to root out these rustlers for us?' Elizabeth Tolliver put in suddenly.

'I'm going to have a damn good try,' Gilby replied, unconsciously fingering the scar on his neck.

'I like men of action,' Elizabeth Tolliver said, as she tried to touch his hand.

Gilby withdrew it quickly. 'I've got to be going,' he said, turning for the door.

As he left, he heard an argument starting inside. Ahead of him, he saw Kathy looking in the window of a nearby shop. He hurried to catch up with her.

She turned, as she saw his reflection in the window.

'I see you got out as fast as you could,' she said, with a pleasant smile.

'She sure is something, that Elizabeth Tolliver,' Gilby said, as they walked in the direction of his office.

'I saw the mayor a couple of hours ago,' Kathy said suddenly. 'He said you needed someone to clean out your office.'

'That's true,' Gilby said, as they walked down the street.

'I'd like to try for it,' Kathy said.

Gilby looked at her. 'You?' he said, in surprise.

'Sure, I'm a widow and need the money,' she said, with a tight-lipped smile.

'Fine. Let's get down there, and I'll show you the place.'

Kathy followed him down to the office, and waited while he fished out the keys that Al Starret had given him.

'It sure looks a mess,' Kathy said with a smile. 'Then Norman wasn't the greatest housekeeper in the world.'

'Norman?' Gilby asked, opening the windows again.

'Norman Reece. Your predecessor,' Kathy said.

Sitting at the desk, Gilby asked her, 'What happened to him?'

'Rustlers shot him. He was out chasing them on the edge of the Flying G land, and they bushwhacked him.'

Gilby thought for a moment, and said, 'How do you know they were rustlers?'

'Dennis Morgan saw them driving off some of the cattle. He saw Norman chasing them, and found his body later near Ryker's Creek.'

'Anybody ever catch any of these rustlers?' Gilby asked.

Kathy shrugged. 'No. But old Isaiah Parker reckons the good Lord's got a hot spot in Hell waiting for them.'

'Isaiah would think that, wouldn't

he?' Gilby grinned uncomfortably.

'Al Starret said you had a run in with Isaiah, and were lucky to live to tell about it. Isaiah and the Lord are firm friends.'

'It might be Isaiah who gets there first, if he isn't careful.'

'More than one have said that.' Kathy looked round the dusty office. 'Where do you want me to start?'

Gilby ran his gaze round the room. 'Wherever you want. You can start in the morning; I'll fix it up with Al.'

'See you in the morning then,' she said, and went out.

When she had gone, Gilby started to fix himself a pot of coffee.

Something about Elizabeth Tolliver nagged at his mind. Maybe he just didn't like her. He thought about it while he sat drinking his coffee, the door of the office standing open to let in some fresh air. Looking back, he realized that she reminded him of Mercy, and something that he would never believe about her. She and

Elizabeth Tolliver looked at men in the same way, he suddenly realized.

After a while he heard a footstep on the boardwalk outside, and Elizabeth Tolliver came into his office.

'Hi, Frank,' she said, with a friendly smile.

'Mrs Tolliver,' he said, getting up.

She beamed at him. 'Elizabeth, please,' she said.

'I think I'll stick to Mrs Tolliver,' he told her. 'I think it's going to be better that way.'

She bridled at this, and for a moment the smile disappeared.

'What can I do for you, Mrs Tolliver?' he asked her.

'I'm on the church committee,' she said, edging up close to him, until their bodies brushed.

Gilby took a step away from her, but she followed him.

'We're having a dance in the church hall on Saturday night, and since you're our new sheriff I thought we might invite you along to welcome you.'

The invitation took Gilby by surprise, Elizabeth Tolliver didn't look like the kind of woman you found on church committees. He moved further away from her, but she edged closer.

'I can't say just now,' he replied, feeling the heat from her. 'It depends on how quiet the town is.'

'You don't look like the kind of man who can pass up on some fun,' she said, leaning forward, and showing him her cleavage.

'I'm not, Mrs Tolliver, but the town pays my wages.'

'I appreciate that, Sheriff, but — '

As she was speaking, her husband came into the office, not looking any too pleased when he saw her.

'I thought you were looking after things in the store,' she said, going red in the face with anger.

'I was getting worried about you,' he replied sarcastically.

'You can see I'm in good hands. The sheriff's agreed to come to the church dance on Saturday night.'

The lie shook Gilby. He opened his mouth to deny it, but her husband beat him to it.

'Doesn't take you long does it, Elizabeth?' he said, getting redder.

'I don't know what you mean,' she stormed at him. 'I was just being friendly, that's all.'

'I bet Kathy's husband knew how friendly you could be,' Tolliver yelled, making to hit his wife. A trickle of spittle ran down his chin.

Getting between them, Gilby put his hand on Jack Tolliver's arm.

'Cool down,' he advised him. 'I've got a couple of empty cells down there that haven't been used for a while. One of them could just about accommodate you.'

Jack Tolliver simmered down straight away. He relaxed and the colour left his face.

'All right, Sheriff,' he muttered. 'All right.'

'Thank you, Sheriff,' a smug sounding Elizabeth Tolliver put in.

Jack Tolliver turned and stormed out of Gilby's office. A few minutes later, his wife followed him. Watching them go, Gilby shook his head and sat down.

'I've just been nearly run down,' Al Starret said, a few moments later when he walked into the office.

'You mean the Tollivers?' Gilby asked him.

'Sure I mean the Tollivers,' Starret replied, with a laugh.

'They're an odd pair,' Gilby said speculatively.

'You can say that again. They came here about a year or so ago from a place called Chantry and opened up the emporium.'

'Chantry?' Gilby mused.

'You know them?' Starret said, as he sat down to take the weight off.

'I guess not. I thought I knew the woman, but it wouldn't be from Chantry,' Gilby said, taking out the makings.

'Kathy might be able to help you there,' Starret told him.

'How do you mean?' Gilby leaned forward on the desk as he put a match to the stogie.

'They found her husband dead in Elizabeth Tolliver's buggy one night, out near the creek that runs behind the town about a mile from here. Of course, it was hushed up. Kathy's a pretty popular woman round here, but she's not stupid, so she might have figured it out.'

The smoke from Gilby's stogie curled upwards. His eyes followed it. He was still watching it when Isaiah and his brood clumped in through the door as Starret left. He and Isaiah looked at each other for a minute.

'I heard they'd got a sheriff,' Isaiah said, with seething anger, looking round at the other two. 'I didn't figure they'd be stupid enough to hire you.'

'Yeah. What in God's name got into this town?' Matthew snarled at him.

'Listen, you mealy-mouth old hypocrite,' Gilby said, coming round the desk, and confronting Isaiah. 'What you did the other day is attempted murder, and unless you behave, I'm going to do something about it.'

Matthew had gone white-faced as Gilby snarled at him, like he wasn't expecting Gilby to jump at him. He looked shaky and frightened. Delilah was hiding a smirk from them all.

'I'd do as he says, Pa,' she said. 'He looks like he means it.'

'I do mean it,' Gilby told her. 'If you want to do something, you'd best help me catch these rustlers.'

'Just so long as you do something about them when you do catch them,' Isaiah told him. 'Don't want any lily-livered jury letting them get away with it.'

'I'll do something about it, along with the courts and not you and your rope. Now, let's start at the beginning. Show me on the map over here where you found the sheriff's body,' he said, going over to the wall.

Isaiah followed him across, and put a bony finger to the map.

'Right here,' he said, pointing to a spot marked Ryker's Crossing.

Gilby followed his finger. 'What's up here?' he asked, looking beyond the Crossing.

'Open land. Nobody owns it, it's just empty land,' Isaiah told him.

'I'll get up there this afternoon,' Gilby said, taking a look at the clock on the wall. Al Starret had had it cleaned and fixed up.

'That sounds all right to me,' Isaiah said. 'Me an' Matthew are gonna be in town fixin' to get some more money off the bank. I ain't sure they're gonna let us have it, though.'

'If yer gonna be doin' that,' Delilah said, 'I'll get back to our place an' see if I can round up any more strays. Them rustlers might have dropped some.'

'Take a good look down here,' the Bible-belter said, pointing to the edge of the map.

'OK, Pa,' Delilah said, giving Gilby an extra friendly smile and going out of the office.

9

For a while, Gilby stood staring at the map, then left the office and locked the place up, and headed down to the livery.

'You got my horse?' he asked the livery man.

'Sure have. Give me a minute and I'll get her saddled up for you.'

A few minutes later, he led Gilby's horse out into the yard and handed him the leathers. Once he got into the saddle, Gilby headed the horse up to Ryker's Crossing. The weather was hot, and soon the sweat was trickling down the back of his neck.

He headed up the draw that led to the Crossing and hauled on the leathers at the top. He looked down on to the slow-moving water that ran down the riverbed. Gilby kicked his horse and rode down to the edge of the water. For a while he looked round, but could see nothing. A wave of bitterness came over him. Another lawman bushwhacked and nobody seemed to give a damn.

On the other side of the water, the trail led upwards between a couple of hills. The flies kept on licking at his face and tormenting his horse as he rode. At the top of the trail, he looked down into a grassy bowl filled with trees. That was as good a place to start looking, he reckoned. When he had ridden down the trail he moved in among the trees. The place was peaceful and quiet except for the buzzing of the flies and the birds up in the trees.

A cabin appeared just beyond the trees with a line of smoke crawling up into the sky. Hitching his horse to a tree, he drew his .45 and made his way towards it. As he was nearing it the door of the cabin opened and a man came out holding a carving knife in front of him. Glancing back, Gilby could see that he had come too far to go back, the only thing he could do would be to move in among the herd and hope that nothing spooked it.

The man was big, with a bushy black beard. He moved awkwardly as he got to the herd. By this time, Gilby had holstered his gun, and was on the herd's outer edges, wondering if it had been a good idea, but it was too late to change his mind now. The man was going into the herd instead of taking one from the edges.

From behind one of the beeves, Gilby watched him as he grasped the horns of the steer and tried to lead it away. The steer skittered, and kicked backwards. His captor panicked and tried to pull him away. It lost its temper, and snorted loudly. Behind him, Gilby knew that the other beeves were getting scared. By now he himself was well in the herd, with no easy way out. The dust was starting to rise from where the steer that had been picked for the table and his captor were struggling.

The rest of the herd was starting to

move. Gilby grabbed the horns of the nearest and swung on to its back. The longhorn squirmed as Gilby got up there, but Gilby held on. The herd was starting to bellow and run over the grassy ground. From the corner of his eye, Gilby watched as the man with the carving knife, went down under the hooves. The sound of the stampeding beeves drowned out his last screams.

Gilby was hanging on to the horns of the steer knowing that if he slipped off it would be the end of him. The pace of the stampede became faster and faster. The animal tried everything it knew to get Gilby off its back. They were out of the bowl now and heading across a flat plain that stretched as far as the eye could see. The herd ran on, seeming to Gilby endlessly. Every bone in Gilby's body was being shaken until he felt that it would burst out through his skin. His sight became blurred, and he felt like his breakfast was coming up.

Trees started to appear on either side of him, but at last he felt the speed of the stampede begin to slow. Gradually, the longhorn became tired and found its way out of the rest of the herd, slowing to a leisurely walk, its head down ready to chew at the grass. It stopped finally under a low branched tree.

Quickly, Gilby swung down, his body aching, the muscles in his legs shaking where they had clung on to the side of the beef. A few yards away stood a tree. Worried in case the animal or the others started to stampede again, he caught hold of the lowest branch and clambered into it. For a while he lay in the branches, watching the steer chomping at the grass, while its fellows did the same nearby.

After a time, Gilby could make out four riders headed his way. The rustlers were coming for the beeves that had stampeded, he figured, pressing himself into the branches and hoping they wouldn't see him. Below him, he could hear them talking, and watched as one of them took a bottle from his saddle-bag and took a pull at it. They started to round up the herd. Gilby held his breath while they went about it. When they had got the herd together they started to drive it back in the direction of the cabin. He stayed where he was until they were out of sight.

When he got down, he fell to the ground, his legs still shaking with the pressure he had had to exert to stop himself coming off the steer. He lay there looking up at the sky, every bone in his body aching. In the end he decided that he couldn't stay where he was forever, and dragged himself to his feet. A lot of the shaking had gone from his legs, and his stomach felt better.

He looked towards the horizon and wondered how far it was to Centreville. A good few miles he guessed. There was nothing for it, but to start walking. Watching the sun, he knew in which direction to head. As he walked, he kept his eyes open for any sign of the rustlers. Gilby had walked for an hour when he saw something ahead of him.

Drawing his gun, he looked round for some cover. A mess of rocks stood off the trail. Taking cover behind them, he watched a rider leading her horse.

'Hold up,' he shouted, as he recognized Delilah, who was leading her lame horse.

She looked at him in surprise.

'Hold up yourself,' she said.

'Looks like you're in the same kind of mess as I am,' he said, putting his gun away.

'I like a man who likes exercise, but it is a fair way to town.' She stopped and faced him.

It took Gilby a few minutes to tell her what had happened.

'You was damn lucky,' she said, chewing a stalk of grass as they walked.

'I had to find out where they're holed up,' he said.

'You think they're gonna be there when we get back to town and get a posse out here?' she asked him.

'No, but it's a start to getting them out of the territory. Now, they've got to

107

find somewhere else to hide.'

'That's right, but we've got to find somewhere to hide for the night. We ain't gonna make it back to town, an' it gets pretty cold out here.'

'Don't suppose you've got a hotel handy?' Gilby asked her, with a smile.

'No, but there's an old shack up here a ways. We could bed down there for the night,' she said, giving him a sideways glance. After they had been walking for another half an hour, she led him up a narrow trail with clumps of trees on either side. The cabin appeared in the gloom.

'Wait here,' Gilby said to her, putting his hand on her shoulder and drawing his gun.

The cabin had a spooky air in the dark, and seemed empty. Gilby cat-footed towards it, and prowled round for a spell. Then he kicked the door open and looked inside.

'We're OK, it's empty,' he told her.

When they got inside she asked him if he had any matches. Gilby rooted round in his pocket and pulled out a box. Striking one he could see that the place was practically falling down.

'At least there's a lamp,' Delilah said, straightening out her black hair and cleaning out the cobwebs that were tangled up in it.

Striking another match, Gilby went over to the lopsided table and put it to the lamp. For a few seconds the lamp spluttered, but then the wick took and the lamp lit.

Delilah picked it up, and shone it round the cabin.

'Just like I remembered it,' she said. 'Just surprised there was something still in the lamp to light. You got anything to eat?' she asked him.

Gilby searched in his pockets then laughed. 'I guess not.'

'You just sit here. I've got something in my saddle-bag. It ain't much, just stale sandwiches I brought out with me, and stuff for making coffee,' she said.

'Looks like there's a rusty pot for making coffee in here,' he replied, picking up the pot from the fireplace in the corner.

Gilby cleaned off the coffee pot and started to build up the wood from the pile in the fireplace, ready for Delilah to come back with the sandwiches and water from her canteen.

When she returned, Gilby put a match to the fire. It took a couple of matches before the wood started to smoke, then burn. Delilah opened the paper parcel and handed him one of the sandwiches.

'Thanks,' Gilby said, taking one, as he put the pot with the water on the fire to boil. When the coffee had been made it was completely dark, and the shadows from the fire were dancing on the wall. Outside the wind had started to get up, and it was becoming colder.

'Well, we've gotta face it,' Delilah began by saying.

'Face what?' Gilby asked her.

'You're a man and I'm a woman, and there's only one bed, and I guess you ain't that much of a gentleman.'

With a grin Gilby got up. She was right: he wasn't that much of a gentleman.

In the morning, Gilby walked round to the back of the cabin to bring Delilah's horse round when he heard horsemen cantering up to the cabin. He pulled himself right up against the wall and inched around to the front of the cabin, gun in hand. There were four men arguing with Delilah.

'Just what the hell's yer ol' man doing?' a thick-set fella in a check shirt demanded of Delilah.

'He's just protecting his land like the rest of you would protect yours, Josh Carter,' she shouted back.

'You tell him to steer clear of my land, or he'll git a bullet, and that goes for your no-good brother Matthew. We ain't got no quarrel with you, Delilah,' Carter finished up by saying.

'Then maybe you've got a quarrel with me,' Gilby said, stepping out from the side of the cabin.

Carter and his boys turned to face him.

'Who the hell are you?' Carter demanded, before he had seen the star on Gilby's vest.

'Sheriff of Centreville,' Gilby said quickly, waggling the gun at the men.

'It's her ol' man we've got a beef with,' Carter went on.

'Why, what's he been up to?' Gilby asked him, putting his gun away.

'He's been out on my land,' Carter said, holstering his own gun. 'Prowling about like he owns it, him an' that boy of his, Matthew. Took a shot at a couple of new fellas I took on. Scared the hell out of them.'

'Yeah, the old coot ought to be locked up,' the fella on Carter's right said, running his sly eyes over Delilah's body.

'Just who are you?' Gilby asked him.

'Ben Garnet, foreman of the Wild Horse spread. Mister Carter's my boss,' Garnet replied, staring dangerously at Gilby.

Gilby knew that if he was going to have trouble with any of them, it would be Garnet.

'If you want to make something of this, you put the gun away and I'll take off my star,' Gilby said.

For a minute, both men faced each other in silence, then Garnet's nerve broke and he put the gun back in its holster.

'I guess I'll let it ride, for now,' he said to Gilby.

'Get about your business,' Gilby said to them.

Without another word they mounted up and rode out.

'Your pa get into a lot of trouble?' he asked Delilah, when Carter and his men had gone.

'Some,' she said, watching the dust disappear to the east.

'He's just gonna have to be careful. If he does to anybody else what he did to me, I'm gonna bring him and Matthew in, and you if you're in with them,' he told her.

'I didn't want no part of that branding. I'm all fer hanging rustlers. They've cut down our herd by a good half. If you don't catch them or stop them, we'll have nothing left,' she said bitterly.

'Just remember what I told you,' Gilby said threateningly.

10

'Just where the hell have you bin,' Isaiah stormed, when they came walking into the yard of the Broken Spur later that morning.

'I ran into a neighbour of yours,' Gilby said to the old man.

'What neighbour would that be?' the rancher asked him.

'Fella called Josh Carter,' Gilby said.

'Him?' rasped out the old man, spitting into the dust.

'Yeah, him,' Gilby told him. 'Looks like you're pretty damn quick with yer rifle, like you've bin with yer rope. It's gonna stop and it's gonna stop now,' Gilby said watching Matthew.

Isaiah ignored him and looked at Delilah.

'I asked you where you've been?' the old man repeated.

Delilah dropped the leathers of her

horse. 'I've bin looking fer strays like I said I would.'

Isaiah's face went red with rage, and he reached for the whip which was hanging over the rail of the corral. He fed it through his hands and raised it. Delilah held up her arm to fend off the blow. Gilby pushed her out of the way, and threw himself low, tackling Isaiah round the legs. They both fell into the dust, Isaiah beating at Gilby's back. Matthew licked his lips, his eyes glowing as the two men fought. Gilby got his arms round his waist and somehow struggled to his feet. For all the thinness of his body and arms, Isaiah was a strong man. He shook Gilby off and ran at him before Gilby could regain his breath. He struck Gilby in the chest with his shoulder, and Gilby reeled back, the air driven out of his lungs. The rancher ran at him again, but Gilby moved to one side and left his foot in the way. Isaiah fell over it but recovered quickly, and got to his feet, ready for Gilby's rush. Gilby came at him, then stopped and feinted at Isaiah's head. Isaiah went for it, then Gilby unleashed a powerful left to the stomach, folding him over.

As Isaiah lay on the ground, Matthew came running across from the corral. He threw himself at Gilby, his eyes gleaming with rage and hatred. Taking a step back, Gilby aimed a blow at Matthew's face. Matthew ran into it, his nose flattened against Gilby's fist, and he fell back in the dust.

Matthew lay stunned, his hand to his broken nose. The sheriff's hands wrapped themselves round his collar and hauled him to his feet. Dragging him to the rail of the corral, he flung Matthew against it and tore the shirt off his back. Behind him on the ground lay the whip that Isaiah had intended to use on Delilah.

'You've had this coming to you,' Gilby said, and brought the whip down on Matthew's back.

Matthew screamed again and again, then slid down the rail to the ground.

Gilby hauled him up and pressed him against the rail and whipped him again, each time opening up another stripe on his back, until the whole thing was a bleeding mess. Then he stopped. Delilah filled a bucket from the trough and threw it over Matthew's back, sluicing off the blood and skin. Matthew lay exhausted in the dust, one arm over the corral bar.

'You got a horse I could borrow for a spell?' he asked the girl.

'Yeah, I'll get you the spare out of the barn,' she said.

'You can pick it up in the livery in town,' he told her, when he got in the saddle.

'Just leave some money at the old livery with the man,' she told him. 'Reckon you won't be seeing your own again.'

'Thanks,' he said, as he started back to Centreville.

★　★　★

When he got back to town he went to see Starret and told him what had happened.

'Round up some men,' Starret said. 'Go up there and see if you can catch them, but I think you're wasting your time.'

'I reckon I will be,' Gilby said.

It took him an hour to round up enough men to go up after the rustlers. As they were riding out, he saw Elizabeth Tolliver watching them from the front of the emporium.

As they rode, Gilby reckoned it was about time that he had a deputy. Maybe Starret knew someone who would take the job on. Maybe.

When they got to the cabin it didn't take Gilby long to realize that Starret was right. The rustlers were long gone. They scoured the area, then headed up country following the tracks left by the cattle. It soon became apparent that the herd was being split up into separate parcels.

'OK,' he said to Starret, 'we ain't got

enough men to fight them if we did catch up with them.'

'We'd best head back then,' Starret said, as Gilby wheeled the posse around and headed back to Centreville, where again he saw Elizabeth Tolliver standing on the step of the store watching them.

'I know the fella you want for a deputy,' Starret said to him, when Gilby mentioned it. They had gone over to Starret's place for some eats and Starret had fixed him a meal.

'I won't be too long,' the mayor said, as he went out leaving Gilby to eat.

Half an hour later, he came back with a tall, young fella.

'This is Mike Blake,' Starret said, introducing him.

'Pleased to meet you,' Mike said, holding out his hand.

'Hi,' Gilby said. 'Let's take a walk down to the office and get you sworn in.'

Blake was quiet as they walked, something Gilby was glad about. He wanted some rest and some time to think about the rustling.

'You've never been in this line of work before?' Gilby asked him, once they reached the office.

'No, sir,' Mike said eagerly.

'First off it's Sheriff, not sir,' Gilby said, tossing him the deputy's star from the top drawer.

With evident pride Mike pinned on the star.

'There's a bunk back there,' Gilby said, pointing to the door at the back of the office. 'I'm gonna get myself some sleep. If there's any trouble, wake me straightaway. Don't try and handle it yourself. Got that?'

'I've got it,' Mike said.

Gilby dropped on to the bunk and closed his eyes.

A few minutes later, the office door burst open. The barkeep from the Painted Cage came in, gasping for air. Mike tossed the newspaper down.

'Yeah?' he asked the barkeep.

'Can you or the sheriff get down to the saloon before all hell breaks loose?'

121

Mike got up and headed for the back. He shook Gilby violently and waited for him to surface, and told him what had happened.

Stretching, Gilby swung himself off the bunk.

'Get me a shotgun,' he said, as he hitched up his trousers.

The barkeep was still waiting in the office.

'What's the matter?' he asked him.

'It's some fellas from the Wild Horse. They got to teasing Delilah, and she took it hard,' the barkeep told him.

'Damn it to hell,' Gilby snorted, as they went out into the street.

The barkeep pushed his way through the batwing doors. Delilah was standing with her back to the bar, her face red and angry. Two men were confronting her. One of them was Garnet.

'What's going on here?' Gilby demanded.

Garnet turned to him. 'We wuz just funning with her, and she smashed a glass in muh amigo's face,' he told him.

'Like hell they was,' the furious Delilah yelled. 'They tried to get me to go outside with them. When I wouldn't, they tried to drag me outside.'

'That's a damned lie, Sheriff. Look at Alec's face. Damn bitch dragged a bottle down it,' Garnet snarled.

The cut was a bad one. The blood was mixing with Alec's stubble. His face was sick-looking.

'Anybody see what happened?' Gilby asked those in the saloon.

For a moment no one spoke.

'She's right,' a fella at the far end of the bar said. 'It was their doing and that Garnet. Alec got what he deserved. They tried to drag her outside.'

There was a murmur of agreement.

'Looks like that's it, boys,' he told Garnet and Alec. 'Let's get down to the jail.'

Garnet and Alec said nothing, but followed Gilby's look in the direction of the batwings.

'You'd better get out of town for the night,' he told Delilah.

'Maybe I will, maybe I won't,' she said.

Ignoring her, Gilby ushered his prisoners through the door and down to the jail.

'Mike,' he called to his deputy. 'Go and get the doc for this fella.'

'OK, boss.'

'Get in there,' Gilby told his prisoners.

Sullenly, they went in to the cells, Gilby took the key and locked them in.

'Make yerselves comfortable until the doc gets here,' he told them.

Alec said nothing, but collapsed on to one of the bunks, holding his bloodied face.

'I'll fix you for this, Sheriff,' Garnet said, with a mean look on his thin face.

'Don't do anything stupid,' Gilby warned him. 'It isn't worth it.'

'We'll see.' Garnet replied, as he slunk over to the free bunk.

It took Doc Bannister ten minutes to get to the jail with his bag.

'Mighty nasty cut you've collected,'

he said to Alec, after he had looked it over. 'Gonna take a couple of stitches to fix it up.'

'Get it over with then,' Alec said morosely.

It wasn't long before the doc had it cleaned up and stitched. 'That's it, gents,' he said, as Gilby let him out.

When he had gone, Gilby confronted the two men.

'I'm going to throw you out in the morning,' he told them. 'Stay out of town for a spell, because if you don't, you'll be seeing the inside of this cell for a lot longer.'

Garnet stood close up to the bars. 'You ain't heard the last of this, Sheriff,' he growled, gripping the bars until the skin of his knuckles showed white.

'Let it go,' Gilby warned him. 'Life's too short, and it might be your life that's shortened considerably.'

Garnet snarled at him as he sauntered back to the office.

11

Elizabeth Tolliver was in the back of the store cleaning the gun she had brought from upstairs. Jack was out front serving the last customer of the day. She wanted the gun cleaned and in the pocket of her dress before Jack came in. Not that she minded what Jack said or did, but it made things simpler if he didn't know. She was going to kill Kathy. Frank Gilby hadn't been in town two minutes before she was making eyes at him. If anybody was going to have Frank Gilby she was. Outside, she could hear Jack closing up for the night. He slid the bolts across and turned the key in the lock. Closing the chamber quickly, she pushed the gun into the pocket of her dress as Jack came in.

'Going out?' he asked suspiciously, as she put on her cloak.

'Just getting some fresh air,' she said,

her green eyes narrowing.

Jack's jaws tightened. 'You got your eye on that sheriff, ain't you?'

She flared in anger. 'If I have so what? You aren't going to do anything about it, are you?'

Jack Tolliver bit his knuckle, knowing she was right. There was nothing he would do about it. He watched her go to the rear door and out into the yard. She was soon lost in the fast falling dark.

Kathy had just left the home of her mother-in-law, and was heading towards her own house. The dark seemed to have fallen faster than usual and she was hurrying along the street, the hem of her skirt trailing in the dust. She had just left the part of town where all the saloons were and which frightened her most, but her mother-in-law was getting on in years and couldn't do things for herself as well as she used to.

Elizabeth Tolliver walked along the street on the opposite side, just behind Kathy. She had seen her crossing the street after she came out of the yard. The best time to take a shot, she reckoned, would be when Kathy got to her house. There was a lamp on the gate that Kathy always lit before she went out; she would be pretty clear in its light. That's when she would shoot her.

After Gilby had had a few hours' sleep, he had sent Mike home to get some rest before he came on in the morning. Taking down a shotgun from the rack, he broke it open and put in a couple of shells. The street was pretty quiet. He took his time going down to the red light district, and had crossed over to where the shops and the two banks were.

Ahead of him, he saw Kathy hurrying to her home. As he was about to call out to her, he saw the flash from a gun, and heard the shot.

Kathy stumbled when the gun exploded from the alley. Gilby tore over towards her and fired a hunk of lead into the alley. Turning, he put his hand under Kathy's arm and helped her to her feet while half dragging her to the alley behind him.

A light came on in the house next to Kathy's and the figure of Colonel Harry Masters, clad in a white nightshirt and holding a Winchester, came out on to the steps.

'I said what's going on out there?' he yelled, raising the Winchester.

'Get back inside,' yelled an angry Gilby.

'You want any help, Sheriff?' the colonel called out again.

'You all right?' Gilby asked the pale-faced Kathy.

'Yes, I'm fine. You'd better go and calm him down.'

Gilby raced across the street, pretty sure that the gunman had gone by now.

'I said get back inside,' he said to the old colonel.

'Anything you say, Sheriff,' the colonel gabbled, allowing Gilby to push him back into the house.

Other people had started to come

into the street to see what had gone on.

'Just go home,' Gilby said, trying to quieten them.

Slowly the crowd drifted away.

'You feeling all right?' Gilby asked the still shaken Kathy.

'I guess so,' she said.

'The best thing for me to do is to see you into the house,' Gilby said, slipping his arm into hers. Once inside he checked to make sure that everything was all right.

'Any idea who that might have been?' Gilby asked her.

'No, I can't think of anybody who would take a shot at me,' she said, taking off her bonnet.

At that moment, Mike came up the steps his gun in his hand.

'Too late for that,' Gilby told him. 'You see anybody who shouldn't be out there?'

Mike shook his head. 'Not a soul, only that dumb old colonel parading up and down on the veranda.'

'If you're OK, we'll be getting back

to the office once we've had a quick look round,' Gilby said.

From the porch, Kathy watched them go, then she went back inside, her hands trembling.

'What do you make of it?' Mike asked Gilby when they returned to the office.

Scratching his head, Gilby shrugged. 'There can't be that many people who dislike Kathy, and there's none I can think of who hates her enough to risk hanging for it.'

'Maybe that's all the excitement you'll get for one night,' Mike replied, heading for the door.

'We'll see,' Gilby replied, watching his deputy leave.

When Mike had gone, he reloaded the shotgun and went out into the street. The place had settled down now. Gilby walked down to the saloons, just poking his head into see if things were all right.

He pushed through the batwings of the Painted Lady, and sensed that something was going on as a hush fell over the place.

'You gonna have a drink with us, Sheriff?' a familiar voice said.

Delilah was lounging against the bar, beside her lounged Michael Goodnight.

'I thought I told you to go home,' he said to her.

'I ain't no little girl,' she said. 'An' I don't think you can make me.' She laughed.

'Yeah, come an' have a drink,' the boy said. 'Now you've scared them rustlers off you deserve a drink.'

'I deserve a break from boys like you,' Gilby said. 'Get back home, and stay away from women like her, or she'll eat you alive,' he said, pointing at Delilah.

Delilah laughed noisily. 'He knows what he's doing, Sheriff.'

'Come on,' Gilby grabbed Michael by the arm and led him outside and pushed him up against the wall. Delilah followed.

'We're gonna take a walk down to the

jail and get you sobered up.'

Michael Goodnight was a trouble-some cuss and it took Gilby some time to get him there. He pushed him into a cell and locked the door.

'What happened to them other two fellas?' Delilah asked him.

'Garnet and his pal?'

'The same,' she answered, tossing her head back and laughing.

'I'll let them go with a warning. Reckon they learned a thing or two,' Gilby said.

'You want to watch that Garnet. He's a mean, low bastard. He ain't gonna forget it.'

'He will if he knows what's good for him.'

'Got Michael safely bedded down?'

'Yeah, he's safely bedded down,' Gilby replied, putting his shotgun on the rack.

'What are you goin' to do with him?' she asked with an impish smile. 'You gonna put him on a chain gang, or just smack his hide?'

Gilby laughed. 'I'm going to get Helena to come and pick him up, once he's sober. She can decide whether to smack his hide or put him on a chain gang.'

'His old man will kill him for giving you some trouble. It's not like when he comes down to see me, messing with the law is different. He don't care about Michael seeing me,' she said with a smile.

'I'm gonna get Helena here in the morning, see if she can do anything with him,' he told her.

'She's welcome to try, but I don't think she will. Anyway, I've got some beer getting warm,' she said, with a husky laugh.

When Mike came on in the morning, Gilby sent him to the Goodnight place. He let the boy stew in the cell, after having gone to see that he was all right.

Garnet and Alec walked silently down the corridor and out into the street when Gilby turned them loose.

'I'm gonna stay in town till my face

feels better,' Alex told Garnet.

'I've sent for yer ma,' Gilby told the surly-faced Michael, when he handed him a mug of coffee.

The boy said nothing in reply. He just looked up at Gilby, his eyes still red.

Helena came into the office with her foreman in tow.

'What's this about Michael?' she asked. Gilby told her, watching her face go white with rage.

'You and that damn Delilah,' she shouted at him, when Gilby brought Michael in from the cell. 'Haven't you got any sense at all? Can't you see she's using you?'

'If she is, it's been a pleasure, and somebody always gets used,' he said, giving Dennis Morgan a look that Gilby couldn't make any sense of, then saw the flicker of fear in Helena's face. Maybe she knew what that look meant.

'All right,' Gilby said, handing Helena the gun that he had taken off the boy.

'I'll tell his pa all about this,' Helena

said, putting the gun in her waistband.

'Just be careful,' Gilby said to the boy. 'Next time you've got drink in you and a gun on your hip, somebody might shoot you.'

Michael scowled at him.

The three of them went out into the street.

'You're not really going to tell Pa, are you?' Michael Goodnight asked, as they rode out of town.

'This time you haven't left me with any choice,' she snapped at him angrily.

'That's a damn shame, because if you do, I'm going to have to tell him about you and Dennis.'

The two looked at him, and each other. They knew that he meant it.

'What the hell are you saying?' Dennis demanded, his hand getting close to his gun.

'I saw you out near the cabin at the old crossing a while back, and I got curious, so I followed you and I've been following you and watching you ever since,' he said, like he'd won a heap of money in a poker game.

'What are you going to do?' Helena's mouth was dry. Dennis Morgan looked frightened.

'Not too much, in fact, I haven't decided yet,' he said, with feigned sweetness, that made Helena grip the pommel of her saddle until her knuckles went white.

'Just be careful,' Dennis Morgan said threateningly.

'No, Dennis,' Helena said her voice full of alarm.

'Don't worry, Helena,' Dennis said, his hand moving quickly away from his gun.

'And there's no need to bother Pa with this, is there? I figure we can both keep a secret.' Michael kicked his horse's flanks and spurred on ahead of them.

'What are we goin' to do?' Dennis Morgan asked Helena.

'Just hope he keeps his mouth shut,' Helena told him, as they rode on to the Flying G land.

12

Garnet had ridden out of Centreville with a chip the size of a mountain on his shoulder. He was going to get even with that tease, Delilah. She had led him on all night. Everybody in the saloon had seen it. His hands tightened on the reins as he rode out. Gilby could wait, but that Delilah was going to get hers first, he decided.

From where the sun was, Delilah would be checking around for any stock that had gone astray near the old mill that his boss had built so they could saw up their own timber from the trees beside the river. They seemed to head for this part of the range, maybe because the grass was better here. Garnet rode easily up the trail.

He hauled on the leathers when he rounded the bend. Up ahead, he could see the ruins of the old saw mill that had burned down during the winter when a couple of drifters taking shelter had got drunk and started messing about with a box of matches and some kerosene. The charred wreck stood out like a mouthful of bad teeth. He swung up the trail following the river.

When he got there, he dismounted and concealed his horse in the burned-out building, and hunkered down to wait. The time passed slowly, and Garnet was starting to wonder if he had missed her. Then he saw her riding the brown horse out of the stand of trees and heading his way. Garnet licked his lips and waited.

Delilah came on, watching the trail carefully for any signs of strays. Ahead of her, the trail seemed quiet and peaceful. Delilah stroked the neck of her horse.

Garnet stood up and stretched as she headed toward him.

What the hell is he doing here? Delilah asked herself, as Garnet stepped on to the trail and raised his hand to stop her.

'What do you want, Garnet?' she asked him, as she got closer.

Garnet shrugged and took a couple of steps nearer.

'Just wanted to say I'm sorry, like,' he said relaxing his stance.

Delilah looked down at him, and thought like hell you do.

Suddenly, Garnet lunged forward and grabbed Delilah's ankle. Twisting it out of the stirrup, he threw her over the other side of the horse. The startled Delilah hit the trail, the breath knocked out of her body.

Garnet ran round the other side of the horse and grabbed her by the shoulders. Quickly, he hauled the struggling girl to her feet and pushed her into the mill.

Recovering, Delilah let out a scream and raked her heels down Garnet's shin. The speed of her recovery surprised him as did the venom of the raking. He yelled and struck out at the girl. The blow only half caught her, but it was strong enough to knock her to the floor.

Garnet moved towards her, a grin of anticipation on his face.

'No sheriff to help you now, you bitch,' he said huskily.

Wild-eyed, Delilah's hands searched round for something to fight him off with.

The scrabbling hands found a piece of wood, sharpened to a point at one end. As Garnet closed with her, she thrust out with her legs. Garnet got tangled up in them, and fell forward on to the stake as Delilah lunged at him with it. His eyes rolled upwards as the blood spurted from his chest. Delilah just got clear of his flailing body. Shaking, she went outside to vomit.

She found Gilby in his office looking over some posters.

'What's the matter?' he asked, as she came in.

'I've killed Garnet,' she told him.

'How'd that happen?' he asked, dropping his pencil.

It didn't take Delilah long to tell him.

'OK, I'll get the body picked up,' he told her.

★ ★ ★

That night, the Flying G boys were half asleep while they were guarding the herd. They figured that it was all over, and the rustlers had taken fright when the sheriff had found their hideout, and come back with a posse. OK, so they hadn't caught them any rustlers, but any longhorn-lifter with half a brain would have got out of the territory.

The boys of the Flying G were wrong. Just after midnight, four of the rustlers came barrelling down out of the hills overlooking the south end of the valley. They rode down, hurrahing and shooting into the air. It took no time at all before the herd was running in the direction the rustlers wanted it to.

One of the guards took a bullet in his belly and fell out of the saddle, throwing his hands into the air, screaming as the piece of hot lead burned his belly. The other drovers weren't any match for Colville's boys. They were cut down by the gun-handiness of the attackers.

Morgan survived the attack like he was supposed to, and rode back to the Flying G ranch house. Helena met him at the door.

'We been hit again?' she asked him, following him into the house.

'How'd they know we moved the herd?' she asked her foreman.

Dennis looked away. 'I dunno, Helena. It was like they knew where they were all the time. Maybe one of the hands is on their payroll.'

'I can't believe that. Did anybody get hurt?' Helena asked, stepping off the veranda.

'Yeah, we lost Muir, and a couple more. They just gunned them down,' Morgan said.

A look of puzzlement crossed Helena's face.

'It's twice we've been hit. Both times we moved the herd, and both times they've hit us.'

Dennis looked at her, and shrugged. 'Like I said, maybe one of our men is on their payroll. Coincidence? That and pure damn bad luck.'

Helena looked at him, and hoped he was right. Even a ranch like the Flying G couldn't afford many more losses. It was especially galling after everybody thought the rustlers had been run out of the area.

'I guess we're going to have to see what Gilby has to say about all this,' she said.

'I guess so,' he replied, walking his horse over to the bunkhouse.

Morgan roused the fella who looked after the horses and got him to saddle one for Helena.

By the time they got to Centreville, Helena's temper hadn't improved much.

'I thought you'd run these rustlers out of the territory,' she stormed at

Gilby who gave her a blank look.

'They hit our herd again,' Morgan put in. 'And killed Muir and a couple of other hands. Up near the end of the trail where it joins up with the Wild Horse spread. Try going up here, near Broken Rock Bend,' Morgan said, his finger on the map.

'Damn it,' Gilby swore. 'I'll go out there and pick up their trail; see if I can track them down.'

'Fine,' Helena said. 'Just do a better job than you did last time.'

'I will,' Gilby's voice was angry and tight.

The three of them went out of the office.

'You go back to the ranch,' Morgan said to Helena. 'I've got a couple of things I've got to do in town.'

'OK,' she said, when Gilby had ridden away. 'Just remember, the captain won't be home tonight, so come up at the usual time.'

'Sure, honey,' Morgan said, without much enthusiasm.

Helena watched him as he led his horse away. Something was wrong with him. Maybe he was getting tired of her. She hoped not. There was nobody else on the ranch she could turn to.

Morgan left his horse outside the new café, and went to get some grub. He reckoned he'd give Gilby an hour to get to the place where he wanted him. He would have enough time to eat, then get up to Broken Rock Bend and put a bullet in Gilby.

The heat was getting to Gilby as he rode up the trail. The sweat ran down the back of his shirt and made it stick to his skin. Pulling off his hat, he mopped his brow with his bandanna. Then, ahead of him up in the blue sky, he saw the first inklings of the storm coming in. A high, black cloud was forming from nowhere, coming up pretty fast. It gathered up like it was being driven by some force that Gilby could not see. A shudder ran through the sheriff. He had seen storms like this before and knew what they could be like. Reckoning there wasn't much he could do, he pushed on to his destination, sensing his horse's fear at what was coming. Gilby rode hard, hoping to find some tracks and get an idea of where the steers were being driven.

Dennis Morgan was feeling that the time had come to settle with Gilby, before he latched on to what was going on. Sliding down out of the saddle, he took the Winchester out of its saddle holster and drew a bead on the trail below him. He looked up at the sky. The storm was coming in fast, and it would hit him any minute.

The first heavy drops fell as he saw Gilby pulling his horse to a halt and taking the slicker out of his saddle-bag, and put it on. The sheriff came on up the trail. The first fork of lightning ripped the sky. Morgan swore. He felt that it was too late to change things as he brought Gilby into his sights, and squeezed the trigger. As the hammer fell, a roll of lightning threw his arm.

The bullet went wide, and took a lump out of the tree that Gilby was passing.

Gilby knew straightaway that he had been shot at. He threw himself out of the saddle, his hand reaching for his gun, only to find that it was hampered by the slicker.

Levering another round into the breech, Morgan fired again, but didn't see where the bullet went. Gilby felt it as it passed through the rain and hit the rock behind him. He had hunkered down behind a couple of rocks on the trail and was trying hard to figure out where the shooting was coming from.

Lightning lit up the place and then the dark and the storm came again. In that second, he had seen a figure changing his position, sliding down beside a fresh set of boulders to Gilby's right. By now, the hard-packed dust had been churned into a clinging black mud.

Gilby slithered on along the ground keeping an eye open for any movement. The rain was really coming down now, blinding him, so that he was having a hard time seeing anything. The foul-tasting mud was getting into his mouth.

Morgan had caught sight of Gilby's yellow slicker. He fired off a shot, and saw it churn up a pool of water.

It missed Gilby's head by an inch. The sheriff winced and looked to his right. He could see nothing but the rain hammering down. Another shot rang out amid the sounds of the storm. This time it was wide of his head; nevertheless, Gilby flinched as it went by. The trail lay between him and the gunman. The way things were with the light, he reckoned it was worth making a run for the other side of the trail and finding out who was behind the trigger.

He got to his feet, and ran for the other side of the trail. As Gilby ran, his feet slithered in the mud, and he almost fell, a bullet slicing through the heavy rain where his head would have been. On the far side of the trail, Gilby flung himself into the mud, and waited for another shot. It didn't come.

Morgan had shifted his position. Now he was ahead of Gilby, and still trying to see him with the rain battering his face. Squinting, he wiped the water out of his eyes, and levered another round into the breech of his Winchester. Reckoning there was no point waiting for Gilby, he moved down through the storm-battered undergrowth, his squat body leaning into the driving wind, his rifle held out in front of him, his eyes squinting against the rain.

The fork of lightning crossed the sky again and he saw Gilby crouching. He knew he had to be quick. Morgan fired from the hip, and watched Gilby fall.

⋆　⋆　⋆

Jack Tolliver watched his wife talking to Kathy in the store. He knew that she had tried to kill Kathy the previous night, and would try again. There was nothing he could do about it. They both knew that. Kathy picked up her bag and went to the door and out into the street. Elizabeth watched her go out into the rain.

'You goin' after her again?' he asked her, the sweat popping out in his forehead. His hands were shaking.

'You've seen how she looks at Frank Gilby,' his wife told him.

'For God's sake, Elizabeth. Wasn't what happened before enough for you? We had to run last time and I figure we're going to have to run this time.' He swallowed hard.

She looked at him with contempt in her eyes. 'You were always so scared, Jack. I don't know what I ever saw in you.'

'You got involved with me, because my family had some money and you wanted to get your greedy hands on it. They were big in Chantry.' His voice was rising to a high pitch.

She stepped back and gave him a pretty cool look.

'You're too damn nervous,' she laughed. 'And remember, if I hang, you

151

hang alongside me.'

She turned and walked quickly away from him.

*   *   *

Morgan fired a split second after Gilby slipped and fell. He hit his head on a rock. The sound of the rain and the storm faded into blackness.

Morgan watched him fall, feeling satisfied with himself. He was pretty sure the lawman was dead. Grinning to himself, he walked back to his horse which he had left tethered behind some rocks just above the trail. Wiping the rain off the rifle, he pushed it into the saddle holster, mounted up and rode back to the Flying G.

13

The rainwater washed the blood from Gilby's head as he lay unconscious in the mud. The lightning continued furiously with no sign of letting up. Inch by inch he came round, his eyes opening slowly, the water washing the mud off the side of his face. Shakily, he got up, and held on to a tree until he felt better. Groggily, he looked round. A bolt of lightning lit up the clearing to show his horse on the far side of the trail, still with its leathers caught up in the scrub. It nickered as he came close to it and put his hand on its mane to reassure it. Gilby put his foot in the stirrup, and hauled himself into the saddle. The horse moved slowly when he touched its flanks with his spurs.

The first thing he saw when he got back to town was the crowd round the door of his office. He eased his way through to find Mike and Starret in there.

They both looked at him in surprise.

'What the hell happened to you?' Starret asked quickly.

'Got bushwhacked,' Gilby told him, dropping into his chair. 'Any coffee in that pot?'

Mike got up from his chair and went over to the pot-bellied stove. 'Sure there's some,' he said, filling a mug for Gilby. 'You'd better get some dry clothes on as well.'

Gilby pulled at his clothes as though he hadn't noticed them until then.

'What's going on out there?' he asked, as Mike passed him the coffee.

'Somebody took another shot at Kathy,' he said. 'Don't worry, they missed.'

Gilby had taken a long swallow of the coffee. 'Just tell me what happened,' he said.

'Kathy had been visiting her husband's mother when somebody took a shot at her, just like last time,' Mike said, as he sat down again.

'Anybody get a look at him?' he asked, not really expecting an answer.

'No, nobody saw anything. Just a shot out of the alley.'

'That's the second,' Gilby said, nursing the mug.

'Any time now that somebody's going to get lucky,' Starret said.

That same thought had struck Gilby, and he didn't like it. He was starting to think more and more about Kathy.

'We'll have to do something,' he said.

'A twenty-four hour guard is out of the question,' Starret said quickly, seeing the way Gilby's mind was turning. 'The town can't afford it, and you've got to get these rustlers rounded up. It's what you're being paid for.'

'I know,' Gilby said irritably. 'Where is she now?'

'At home,' Mike replied.

'I'm going to get some dry clothes then I'm going down there.'

'All right,' Starret said. 'Just remember what I said; Kathy isn't the only problem round here.'

'I'll deal with them out there,' the mayor said, as he got up to leave.

When he had gone, Mike filled up Gilby's mug again.

'I've got some clean stuff out back,' Gilby said. 'I'll just get out of these things.'

He went out back while Mike toted a shotgun around the town to make sure things were quiet. Gilby got himself cleaned up and went to see Kathy.

She opened the door cautiously after he had told her who he was. She held a pistol behind her back, but looked shaky with it when she showed it to him.

'Mike told me you didn't get a look at whoever pulled the trigger,' Gilby said, as he sat down in the chair by the window.

'No,' Kathy replied nervously. 'I just saw the gun flash from across the street.'

'Anybody got any reason to want to

kill you?' he asked, leaning forward in the chair.

Kathy shook her head. 'I can't think of a soul,' she said. 'Everybody's been good to me since my husband died.'

'I heard about that,' Gilby replied cautiously, not knowing how Kathy would take being reminded of her husband dying in Elizabeth Tolliver's buggy.

'Don't worry, I know,' she said. 'Everybody tried to keep it from me, but I knew they were having an affair.'

'And you can't think of anybody who would want to kill you?' Gilby asked her.

'Like I told you, there's nobody I know who would want me dead,' she said, biting her knuckles.

They talked for another half-hour, before Gilby realized that he was getting nowhere. He left and walked down to the jail. As he did so, he passed the emporium and happened to glance up at the window. The curtain moved, and for a second he felt that somebody had been watching him. Gilby walked on, his hand hanging loosely at his hip, the memories of the afternoon's ambush making him even more nervous than he had been.

When Mike came back, he turned in for a few hours to get some sleep on the bunk in the back. The morning found him sore and hungry. Starret didn't seem too pleased when he served him up his breakfast.

'You keep your mind on catching them rustlers. Me and Mike will keep an eye on Kathy,' Starret said, putting down his plate of ham and egg.

'I'll keep it in mind,' Gilby told him, as he began to cut up the ham.

Starret left him alone after that and went about serving the other customers. When he had finished, Gilby took a walk down to the Tollivers' place. Elizabeth Tolliver was in the store tidying it up.

'I heard about what happened,

Frank,' she said, throwing her arms round his neck.

Gilby wriggled out of the unwelcome embrace and moved to the other end of the shop. As he did so, Jack Tolliver came in from the back looking pale and nervous.

'Good morning, Sheriff,' he said, his lips dry.

'Morning, Jack,' Gilby said getting up close to the fella. 'You hear about the shooting last night?'

'Sure, I heard something about it,' Tolliver replied, looking even more frightened.

'I can't figure out who'd try to kill Kathy,' Gilby said to him, watching his face closely.

'No, Jack didn't hear anything. We were both in bed,' Elizabeth Tolliver said quickly, coming to stand at Jack's side, her hand holding his.

'No, I didn't hear anything,' the man said, with a dry mouth.

'Well, if you do happen to hear anything, you let me know,' Gilby told them.

When he was outside, he could hear them arguing.

* * *

Dennis Morgan had ridden back to the Flying G feeling pretty satisfied with himself. Ever since they had cut Gilby down from the tree where Isaiah and his clan had been set on hanging him, he had the feeling that Gilby would be the one to make trouble for them. Now Gilby was out of the way he felt a heap better.

Helena was in the front room of the house when he got there.

'Everything go all right in town?' she asked him.

'Yeah, it went fine,' Morgan said, helping himself to a glass of the captain's whiskey.

'You coming up tonight?' Helena asked him. 'He's in Langton until late tomorrow.'

'Sure. I'll be up,' Morgan said finishing his drink.

As he went out, Helena gave him a hard look. Of late, Dennis didn't seem as eager to come up to her room as he once had been. She hoped he wasn't getting tired of her. It was as lonely as hell being married to a man like the captain. She poured herself a drink and sat down with it. Upstairs, she could hear Michael moving about. She wondered how he could have turned out so bad, but then maybe she did know.

A few minutes later he came downstairs, a self-satisfied look on his face.

'I need some money to go into town,' he told her.

'You expect me to give you some?' Helena said, standing up to face him.

'You expect me to keep my mouth shut about you and Dennis forever?' he sneered. 'I ain't doing it for nothing.'

'I don't think you would. It would kill your father,' she said.

'And you don't think what you and Dennis are doing, would? Are you going to give me any money or not?'

Helena took a wad of notes from the bureau, and peeled some of them off. Michael snatched the whole wad from her.

'I need it all,' he said. 'Delilah's becoming expensive these days. And she likes a man with money.'

'You're not a man yet, if you ever will be,' Helena snapped at him.

'I'm a man; ask Delilah,' he laughed, then turned and left the house.

* * *

Elizabeth Tolliver was getting desperate. Twice she had gone out to kill Kathy and twice she had missed. Jack wasn't making things any better. She could see him shaking and falling apart before her eyes. Tonight she would get it right. She would wait for Kathy outside her house, and shoot her as she went in. Jack had gone upstairs taking a whiskey bottle with him. It would be half an hour before he was asleep. That would give her time to get to Kathy's and wait for her. She had been too far away last time, she thought. This time she would get closer.

Elizabeth put on her cloak, and put the .45 in her pocket. The alley was empty and dark as she went into it. Hesitating at the entrance to the street, she had a careful look round before stepping on to the boardwalk.

The saloons were going strong as she went past them, the music loud like the noise of the drinkers and the whooping of the dancing girls. For a moment she stopped, and moved into an alley as a couple of cowboys from one of the spreads outside town came out. They were inclined to argue and talk noisily, as they rolled a couple of stogies.

The time seemed to drag on forever and Elizabeth was afraid that she would miss Kathy, or one of them would come into the alley to take a leak. In the end they tossed their stogies into the trough and headed for the livery stable and their horses.

Leaving the saloons behind her, she headed across town to Kathy's house. It stood in the middle of a block. Just beyond it a tree overhung the sidewalk. She moved behind the tree and took the gun out of her pocket. She heard the swishing of skirts as she drew back the hammer. Her heart pounded as she stepped from behind the tree and pulled the trigger. She watched as the figure fell, clutching at her heart. Without waiting, Elizabeth turned and ran the way she had come.

Kathy was in the back room, doing her needlework when she heard the gunshot outside her house. She looked up startled, dropped her needlework and reached under the chair for her husband's gun, her hand trembling as she went into the hall. The butt of the gun was cold and heavy.

She seemed to stand there for a long time, before she saw the shadow of a figure through the glass. Her thumb slid towards the hammer and she pulled it back.

'Kathy, it's me, Frank,' Gilby called out.

Kathy almost dropped the gun with relief. Going to the door she opened it. Gilby was on the porch with a worried expression on his face.

'Are you all right?' he asked, holstering his gun.

'I heard a shot,' she gasped. 'What was it?'

'Somebody's killed Starret's wife,' Gilby told her.

'Rita Starret dead?' Kathy echoed.

'Somebody put a bullet in her outside your house,' Gilby said, as he came in.

'I was expecting her. I'd just finished some needlework for her.'

Gilby turned as he heard footsteps on the veranda, his gun in his hand.

'Is that Rita Starret lying out there?' Mike asked.

Gilby nodded.

'Hell,' Mike exploded. 'Al thought the sun rose and set on her. He's gonna take it hard.'

'I can't help that,' Gilby replied. 'We're just gonna have to find who did it.'

Al Starret came rushing up the steps of the veranda looking angry and sick.

'What's happened to my wife?' he demanded, his face red with the exertion of running.

Gilby braced himself, and told him.

The mayor's face crumpled, and Gilby thought he was going to collapse.

'Rita,' he kept muttering.

'Can you get him home, Mike?' Gilby asked his deputy.

'Sure, boss,' Mike replied, taking the mayor by the arm, and leading him away.

Gilby went back into the house, and found Kathy staring at her husband's gun. Gently, he took it from her and sniffed. It hadn't been fired.

'I'll take a look round,' he said. 'Then, if everything's all right, I'll get back to the office.'

'I'm going to be fine, but take a look round,' she said.

Gilby went through the house and then through the garden at the back. There was no sign of anybody.

Mike was waiting for him when he got back to the office.

'Find anything down there?' he asked.

Gilby tossed his hat on to a peg and shook his head. 'Not a thing.' He sat down in a chair.

'Think it's the same fella who took a shot at Kathy?' Mike asked him, pouring some boiling water on to the coffee.

'To be honest, I don't know,' Gilby said. 'How's Starret?'

'Pretty damn shaken. I gave him a couple of shots of whiskey and put him to bed.'

Gilby took the mug from him and drank from it.

'Do you think it's the same fella?' Mike asked Gilby.

'I hope so,' Gilby said, putting down the mug. 'Otherwise we've got two of them running round loose in town.'

'Where do we start looking?' Mike asked him.

Gilby thought long and hard for a moment then shook his head.

'I don't know,' he said.

'I think we'd better think of something before Starret pulls himself together,' Mike said seriously. 'Otherwise we'll both be out of a job.'

'You'd better get some sleep,' Gilby said, draining his mug. 'I'll take a turn round town.'

With that, Gilby took Mike's shotgun, broke it open and checked it. The town was quiet as Gilby walked its darkened streets. As he crossed Main Street a familiar voice called him.

'Looking for more trouble?' Delilah said, a mischievous look on her face.

'I've had enough trouble for one night,' Gilby grinned back at her. 'Maybe you've seen something.'

'Maybe I have and maybe I haven't,' Delilah replied, leaning against the wall of the saloon.

Her attitude was nettling Gilby.

'Either you've got something to tell me or you ain't,' he snapped at her.

'You should ask Elizabeth Tolliver what she was doing at this end of town. I mean, it ain't the kinda place you'd find a woman of Mrs Tolliver's standing at this time of night, is it?'

Gilby gave her hard look. 'Either you know something, or you don't.'

'I've done all my talking for now,' she said and tried to push past him.

Barring her way, Gilby was lost for what to do; in the end, he moved to one side to let her pass.

'Thanks, Sheriff,' she laughed.

He watched her go back into the saloon, then walked on. As he went, he thought about what she had said about Elizabeth Tolliver. She was certainly a man-eater, but a killer was something else. When he got back to the office, he turned in for an hour, feeling pretty sure there would be no more excitement.

★　★　★

Jess Miller, the ramrod from the Circle S, got to Gilby's office bright and early the following morning.

'It's happened again, Sheriff,' he stormed at Gilby, a bloody bandage round his head.

'More rustling?' Gilby said to him, pushing his shirt tails into his trousers.

'Yeah, we're gonna have to bury Billy Wingate. An' I came damn close,' he said angrily, fingering the bandage.

'They run off many?' Gilby asked him.

'Thirty maybe forty head. I thought you had this situation under control,' Miller said to him.

'It's just taking a mite longer than I thought it would,' Gilby replied.

'You'd better be shaking yourself up,' the ramrod said angrily. 'We ain't all got big spreads like the Flying G.'

'Yeah, I'd kinda figured that,' Gilby told him. 'Just where is the Circle S?'

The ramrod walked to the map on the wall, and put his finger on a spot near Ryker's Crossing.

'Here,' he said.

'Not far from the Broken Spur or the Flying G land,' Gilby mused.

'Our land runs on to the Flying G spread,' Miller said, pushing his finger up the map.

Gilby looked at the map but said nothing. The Broken Spur land and the Circle S land along with the Flying G land all met at the same place, right where the previous sheriff had collected some lead. Maybe it was a coincidence or maybe it wasn't.

'You come up with anythin'?' he heard Miller ask him.

'No, not right now,' Gilby answered truthfully.

'Well, maybe you should start earnin' yer money,' Miller said to him.

'I will,' Gilby answered.

'I've got to get back, I've a funeral to fix up,' Miller said, leaving the office.

When he had gone, Gilby looked at the map again. Two of the biggest losers had land in pretty well the same place.

Was it a coincidence, he wondered again.

Half an hour later, Starret came into the office. He was white-faced and, despite the whiskey that Mike had given him, didn't look as though he had slept much.

'You got that murderin' son of a bitch yet?' he demanded.

'Give me time, Al,' Gilby pleaded.

'My wife's dead, an' you're asking for time,' the mayor practically exploded.

'Damn it, Al, you're starting to sound like Parker,' Gilby shouted back.

The mayor said nothing.

'You're right,' he said finally. 'But what about yer friend Kathy?'

'What about her?' Gilby asked in surprise.

'Rita was shot outside Kathy's house,' Al said unreasonably.

'Did it occur to you that whoever shot your wife might be the same fella who shot at Kathy?'

Al stared at Gilby, but said nothing.

'What about it, Al? I'm not saying it

stands to reason, but it's a fair bet, and what reason would Kathy have of shooting Rita?'

The question stumped the mayor. 'None that I can think of,' he said in the end.

They were both silent.

'All right,' Gilby said. 'Then that leaves us back where we started. Somebody shot at Kathy and murdered Rita.' He saw the pained look on the mayor's face at the use of the word 'murder'.

'I'll give you some time to think about it,' the mayor said. 'But I want Rita's murderer caught. I don't care who it is.'

14

Elizabeth Tolliver was in the bedroom, shaking. She knew the moment she had fired the shot that it was not Kathy she had hit. She had seen Rita Starret's face screwed up in pain as she fell with a bullet in her heart. The shock of what she had done had almost made her fall. She knew how much Al Starret cared for his wife and she knew of his past, and she knew what he was capable of.

'Are you satisfied?' Jack asked her from the door of the bedroom.

'It's gonna be like Ralston again, ain't it?' he demanded, leaning against the door. 'We were damn lucky to get out of there without getting hanged.'

When she did not answer he walked downstairs. Elizabeth ignored him, but when she heard the bottom step creak, she reached into the drawer and took out a bottle of whiskey. A good stiff drink calmed her down. She swore at Jack for a spineless coward and put the cork back into the bottle. In the living-room, Jack Tolliver was sitting in the chair facing the window.

It had been the same in Ralston, only there it had been the man who owned the big ranch. They had been lucky to get out and disappear before the mob got ropes round their necks. Jack Tolliver ran his finger round his collar, and sweated a little. It had been worse in the place before: Chantry, the place where they had met and grown up. The thoughts and memories made him shudder.

⋆　⋆　⋆

Brad Colville met Dennis Morgan by the bend in the river just on the Flying G land.

'Got your money, Dennis,' he said, handing the foreman a wad of greenbacks.

'Thanks, Brad,' Morgan said, stuffing

the money in his vest pocket.

'Got anything else for me?' Colville asked, digging out the makings and rolling himself a smoke.

'No,' Morgan said with a shrug. 'I guess we'd better let things lie for a spell. I tried to plug Gilby like I plugged the last lawman, but I didn't make it.'

'Damn shame,' Colville said. 'We could use some more of the folding stuff. I've been thinking it's time to be getting out of this part of the country.'

'Maybe you're right,' Morgan said, fidgeting with the leather of his horse. 'I think if we get rid of Gilby things might cool down some.'

'Maybe you're right,' Colville mused. 'But be careful, I don't want this messing up. We've done OK up to now.'

'I'll get him next time,' Morgan promised his boss.

Morgan rode away from the meeting trying to figure a way to make good on his boast.

★ ★ ★

Gilby was sitting in his office thinking about Elizabeth Tolliver. Just before he rode out of his last job, he seemed to remember something about a man and a woman and a disappearance. He rolled the pencil between his fingers. A few minutes later, he scrawled a message to the Sheriff of Chantry and sent a copy to Ralston, then he walked down to the telegraph office and watched the clerk tap out his message.

'It might be a couple of days, Sheriff, before we get a reply. There's been some rough weather and it's brought the wire down somewhere,' the clerk told him, handing Gilby his copy of the message.

'Thanks,' Gilby said, and headed back to his office.

Elizabeth Tolliver met Gilby on the street while she was going to pick up some groceries. She gave him a sweet, innocent smile.

'Good morning, Frank,' she cooed at

him. 'Remember, we're having a dance at the church hall on Saturday night. Perhaps you'd care to come along and meet some of the townsfolk. You'll find out that there are some good people in this town. Remember I asked you a while back?'

For a minute Gilby was going to say no, but then he thought better of it.

'I'd like that, Mrs Tolliver. I think it would be a good idea to meet some of the townsfolk,' he said with a smile he didn't feel.

'Can't you bring yourself to call me Elizabeth?' she smiled.

'I'll try,' Gilby said, his teeth on edge.

Jack Tolliver almost exploded when his wife got back and told him what she had done.

'It's no harm,' she said soothingly to him.

'What have you got in mind?' he demanded.

'Nothing, just being friendly,' she said to him.

Her husband sneered at her. 'Being

friendly like you were with Kathy's husband.'

'Kathy's husband,' she said with a dismissive shrug. 'I'll never know what he saw in that little mouse.'

'Well, whatever he saw, I think Frank Gilby has seen the same thing,' Jack Tolliver said sharply.

He watched as his wife's face turned white.

'Whatever she saw in him, she'd better take a good look, as she won't be seeing it for long. I'll get the bitch.'

Jack Tolliver's insides turned to mush. He had heard that tone of voice in Ralston.

'Leave it alone,' he yelled at her.

She turned to look at him with contempt all over her face.

'I'm not going to leave it alone until I've got her,' she said venomously.

Jack looked at her with fear in his eyes.

'You looked like that in Ralston when you thought the law was coming for you,' she laughed callously.

Jack held the arms of the chair.

★　★　★

Dennis Morgan rode into the yard of the Flying G. Maybe it was time to get out, and he knew where he could get some money. Colville had thought it was a great idea. Hitching his horse at the rail outside the house, he walked up the steps and went in. Helena looked up, surprised to see him.

'I thought you were out checking some stock,' she said in surprise.

'I gotta a message for you from an old beau,' Morgan said, in a tone that Helena didn't like.

'What old beau?' Helena said uneasily.

'Brad Colville. You remember Brad from that old prison camp?' he said with a sneer that curled up his lips.

A feeling of cold ran through Helena.

'I see you can bring him to mind,'

Morgan went on, resting his foot on the chair.

'What do you know about Brad Colville?' she asked.

'He wants to get reacquainted. Not like it was in the old days,' he added quickly.

'What does he want?' Helena asked him.

'He wants to see you,' Morgan said, reaching out for the decanter on the table in front of him.

'Why?' Helena asked him, her mouth dry.

'I ain't rightly sure,' Morgan lied, as he poured himself a glass of the captain's best whiskey.

'How much has he told you?' Helena asked him.

Morgan shrugged. 'I guess me and old Brad had something in common,' he laughed.

'You bastard,' Helena said, aware of the cook in the kitchen and Michael upstairs.

'Don't take it like that, Helena,'

Morgan said, as he refilled the glass.

'Where is he?' Helena demanded.

'Come on, I'll take you to him,' Morgan told her.

They went out into the yard, Morgan waiting while Helena saddled a horse in the barn. When they came out, they headed south. After about an hour's leisurely riding, they came to a narrow canyon. Away from the sun, in its narrow confine, the dark canyon became cold. Helena shivered as they rode on. By degrees, the canyon lengthened until it finally opened out into the sun again.

The land stretched out in front of them, a broad downward sweep of green, broken by clumps of trees. As they moved down, Helena could make out a rough-looking cabin with a string of horses grazing in the corral. As they got nearer, the cabin door opened and a man came out, dressed in shirt sleeves, grey trousers held up by a broad belt with a heavy pistol jammed into the holster. Suddenly, he raised his hand in a friendly greeting as they approached.

'Hi, Helena,' he shouted to her, with a familiar smile.

Helena found it hard to believe that he hadn't changed in the time since their last meeting.

'Brad,' she said, as she slid out of the saddle.

'You haven't changed much either, Helena,' he said with a laugh, as he came towards her.

Brad Colville, the man to whom she had smuggled a pistol in the prison camp, on the promise that he would take her with him, a promise he had reneged on, and used the pistol to put her husband in a wheelchair. The man who was Michael's father.

'Still holding a grudge, Helena?' he asked her.

'What do you expect?' she asked him.

'You're right to bear a grudge,' he said, ushering her into the cabin.

Four men sat at the upturned crate that served as a table. Dog-eared cards were scattered across it, a half-empty whiskey bottle stood in the centre surrounded by tin mugs.

She looked at the four men and recognized one of them.

'Sergeant Brewster,' she said to him.

'You've got a good memory,' Brewster said, with throaty chuckle, as his thick fingers moved the cards about.

'I didn't like you then, and I don't expect I'll like you now,' Helena told him.

Brewster shrugged. 'That's the way it goes,' he sneered.

'Cut it out, Brewster,' Colville said to him. 'We've got some serious business to talk over with Helena.'

'We've got nothing to talk over,' she said to him coldly.

'We sure have,' Colville said with a grin.

'Like what?' Helena asked him curtly.

'Like how much are you going to pay us to get out of the territory?' he laughed.

Helena gave him a curious look.

'We got as many of your cattle as we

want,' Colville said with a laugh.

'Yeah,' Brewster put in. 'Who do you think's been thinning out yer herds, with Dennis's help, of course?'

The shock hit Helena like a blow. She rounded on Dennis.

'You've been telling them where the herds are?' she said.

'Sure, Helena,' he told her. 'You had so much, we had so little. It didn't seem fair.'

Colville and Brewster laughed as he spoke.

'Just what do you want?' Helena asked turning on them.

Colville took out the makings with an exasperating slowness and started to build a cigarette, smoothing the tobacco into a paper.

'Damn it, Brad, what the hell do you want?' Helena shouted at him.

'Dennis was telling me how there's a tidy pile in that safe you've got in yer ranch house. Let us have it and we'll leave you alone for good. That's a promise I'll keep.'

'There's ten thousand dollars in that safe,' Helena told him. 'And I don't have the combination.'

Brewster gave a laugh. 'Dennis says your loving husband gave it to you.'

'No more lies, Helena,' Colville said, putting a match to his smoke.

'He'd kill me.' Helena looked at Morgan. 'You know how he is with money.'

'Don't let it worry you, Helena,' Morgan said with a cruel laugh. 'We all know how much he loves you.'

A sick feeling came over Helena. If Richard knew that she had taken the money from the safe he literally would kill her, wheelchair or no wheelchair.

'Doesn't sound like he's changed a whole lot since the army,' Colville reminded her. 'Was he real hard on you when he found out he wouldn't be leading any more cavalry charges, and the only thing he would be riding would be a wheelchair?'

Helena could well remember the long days of his insane bouts of temper when they finally convinced him that he would never walk again, and that he was condemned to a life in a wheelchair.

'It was your fault,' she said bitterly. 'Escaping so near the end of the war when your cause was lost.'

'Are you sure you don't mean that *your* cause was lost?' he asked her, with bitter sarcasm.

'You promised that you would take me with you,' she said angrily.

'I wasn't going to take you anywhere. The only place I was going was back to my own people so that we could fight you Yankees. Now, are you going to get that money, or do I have to go and ask your husband for it?' he said threateningly.

'You would, wouldn't you?' Helena said, fighting back the tears.

'There's the small matter of our . . . ' he paused deliberately, searching for a word, 'love affair.'

'You'd tell him now after all these years?' she asked him.

'Why not? A man deserves to know the truth about the woman he married,' Colville said sharply.

'Then maybe you'd better know something of the truth. Michael isn't his son, he's yours,' she said quietly.

The noise in the cabin stopped suddenly. Everybody looked from one to the other. Colville dropped his stogie. Brewster flicked the cards off the crate and all over the floor. Even Morgan's mouth dropped a mite.

'I'm a pappy,' hollered Colville, at the top of his voice.

'Yeah, you're a pappy,' Helena told him.

'What's he like?' Colville demanded to know.

'Very much like you,' Helena replied.

'Boss, this ain't getting us out of the territory,' Morgan put in.

'You're right,' Colville said.

'So what are you goin' to do about it?' Morgan continued.

'You take Helena back for the money,' Colville said to him.

'Maybe we could bring the captain back here as well,' Morgan said maliciously. 'You always reckoned you'd like to meet up with him again after all the hard times he gave you and them boys back in that camp.'

'No, the money's what we need. If old Iron Breeches is there bring him back and we'll have a reunion, but otherwise leave it,' Colville said with a bitter laugh. 'But only if he's there, don't go looking for him.'

'Come on, Helena,' Morgan said, prodding her in the back.

'Keep your damned hands to yourself,' Helena told him, her face reddening with anger.

They went out of the cabin and rode back the way they had come.

15

The yard of the ranch was empty when they got back.

'Looks like the captain ain't back yet,' Morgan said, after a quick look in the stable. 'Let's get the money and get out of here.'

They went into the house, and through to the room the captain used as a bedroom and office. The big safe stood in the corner.

'Best hurry up, Helena,' Morgan told her.

Helena bent down at the front of the safe and began to turn the lock. The tumblers fell into place, and the safe came open. Inside, were stacks of greenbacks, all arranged neatly in bundles, according to their denominations. Greedily, Morgan pulled them out.

'Get a bag, Helena,' he told her.

Out in the yard, a wagon rumbled in.

Helena found a bag easily enough, and gave it to Morgan who crammed the notes into it. They were both so engrossed in what they were doing that they didn't hear the wheelchair coming into the room.

'Planning on leaving?' the captain said.

Sam stood behind him, holding the handles of the wheelchair.

'I don't want to have to shoot you, Sam,' Morgan said.

'Glad to hear it,' Sam replied, raising both his hands.

Morgan tied him up.

'What were you planning to do? Rob me and run away with the money,' the captain said from the wheelchair.

Morgan drew his gun, but Helena pushed his hand aside.

'No, don't kill him,' she cried.

'Well, maybe you're right,' Morgan said.

Quickly he went over to Richard and searched him for a pistol.

'I always suspected that something was going on,' Richard shouted at them.

'Keep the noise down,' Morgan advised him. 'I like Sam, and I wouldn't like to have to kill him,' he said, looking at the cook.

'What were you going to do? Run to Mexico? I'd have had men after you in no time at all.'

'No,' Morgan said. 'There's somebody who wants to meet you. An old army friend of yours.'

'An old army friend of mine?' Richard Goodnight echoed, gripping the rims of the wheels.

'Yeah,' Morgan leered. 'Old Brad Colville. Remember old Brad? He put you where you are today.'

The captain's face became enraged and angry. 'Colville? That Southern trash?' he seethed.

'Careful. Remember Sam's out there. Sam has a dislike of bad language,' Morgan said waggling his gun at the captain.

The captain's temper subsided, but Helena could see that he was barely concealing his rage.

'You got that bag?' Morgan said, taking hold of the handles so that he could wheel the chair out into the yard.

They went through the house. Morgan stopped at the front door and looked out. The yard was still empty. He pushed the wheelchair across the yard and up the ramp into the wagon.

From his upstairs window, Michael watched the chair being pushed into the wagon.

'Take it nice and slow, Helena,' Morgan said after they had mounted up.

Helena laid the leathers across the back of the team and they pulled the wagon out of the yard.

In the back, the captain was fretting and fuming. If he ever got any of them, Helena, Morgan and Colville, on the wrong end of his gun, that would be the end of them.

Colville had seen them coming and

was waiting at the door of the cabin for them.

'It's downright nice to see you again, Captain,' he said, as Dennis wheeled the chair down the ramp.

The captain's face was a mask of hatred as he looked at the man who had condemned him to the wheelchair.

'Damn you,' he spat out at Colville.

Colville grinned wolfishly as he stood over the captain. 'Nice to see that you ain't changed all that much now yer in a wheelchair.'

Goodnight gripped the arms of the chair.

'Glad you've got the money, Helena,' Colville said.

Helena threw the bag at him. Colville grinned again. Opening it, he scooped the money out on to the table.

The captain watched every dollar fall out of the bag, his knuckles white on the arms of the chair.

'What do you want?' he asked. 'Apart from my money?'

'Time to pay a few old scores,'

Colville said with a grim smile. 'I can still remember how you treated them boys in that camp.'

'They were prisoners-of-war,' the captain said.

'They weren't meant to be treated the way you treated them,' Colville rasped.

'This ain't getting us out of the territory,' Morgan called to them from the top of the wagon.

'No, it ain't,' Colville replied.

'Hold it there, Brad, see who we've got here,' one of his men called from the edge of the trees.

Colville turned. One of his men was riding behind Michael Goodnight.

'Who's that?' Colville shouted across to him.

'He's your son,' Helena said.

Colville stared at her, his mouth hanging open. 'That's my son?' Colville asked in surprise.

The captain had gone deathly pale. '*His* son?'

'Yes, *my* son,' Colville said, with a

sound of satisfaction in his voice.

The boy looked down at him. 'I knew he wasn't my real pa,' he said with a laugh.

A look of horror came over Helena's face when Michael said this.

'You gonna teach me to shoot?' Michael asked Colville.

'Yeah, sure, I'll teach you to shoot,' Colville said eagerly.

'I won't let you,' Helena said, her face twisted with the shock.

'You ain't in the best position to stop me,' Colville said. 'In fact, you ain't in any position to do anything,' he said to her.

'Go to hell, Brad,' Helena said through the tears.

In his chair, the captain was struggling with his rage. 'Give me my gun,' he yelled.

Brewster and the others laughed at his outburst.

'Ain't in the army now, Captain,' Brewster said. 'You're just stuck in a wheelchair.'

The captain was threshing about, his rage written in his face. 'Damn it, somebody give me a gun,' he screamed again, beating on the arms of the wheelchair.

Colville and the others ignored him. Then Colville walked over to him, his hand resting on the butt of his gun.

'Time to settle a few scores, Captain,' he said.

Helena watched him, knowing what he was going to do. She watched him slowly draw the gun from the leather, and pull back the hammer. The chamber spun. The captain watched him. There was no fear in his face. The gun went off. The lead went into the captain's chest, flinging him back in the wheelchair so that it went over. Colville laughed.

'Your turn now, Helena,' he said, turning the gun in her direction.

'Damn you, Brad,' she shouted. 'I hope you burn in hell.'

She closed her eyes and waited for it. There was the sound of a shot, and a scream. Feeling no pain, she opened her eyes cautiously. Colville was staggering back, his face turning white as he did so, his eyes rolling upwards. She turned to the clump of trees as another shot rang out. Brewster clutched his throat and fell. Morgan followed him down, clutching at his belly, death written in his face.

Gilby came riding out of the trees, his smoking Winchester across his saddle bow, behind him came Isaiah, Matthew and Delilah looking pretty pleased with themselves.

16

'There's a fella in your office,' Mike told Gilby, when he rode in with the prisoners. 'Name's Jess Walters from Chantry.'

Gilby's face took on a look of interest. 'I'd better get inside and see what he wants. You bring these boys in.'

'OK, boss,' Mike said, hauling the remaining rustlers out of their saddles.

Jess Walters was a heavy-set hard-faced man. He got up and extended his hand when he saw Gilby.

'I got your wire,' he said, crushing Gilby's hand. 'Seems like you've saved me a heap of trouble.'

'Hope so,' Gilby said shaking the coffee pot as Mike led in the prisoners, and took them to the cells

'The descriptions match the folks I'm looking for,' he said, settling himself into the chair. 'They in town?'

'In the emporium,' Gilby said, filling the coffee pot with water.

'Emporium?' Walters asked in surprise.

'Yeah,' Gilby said absently. 'They came into town before I was sheriff, and opened the place up.'

'Let's get down there and see if it's them,' Walters said eagerly.

His eagerness surprised Gilby. 'I'm just going to have some coffee first. Care for a mug?'

'No, thanks,' Walters said quickly. 'Let's just get down there. I've got a big case coming up and I've got to get back.'

'I won't take long,' Gilby said, glancing at him out of the corner of his eye while he poured boiling water on the coffee. He settled back to drink. Walters seemed pretty impatient to get down to the emporium. When he had finished, Gilby got to his feet; Walters did the same, his hand pressing at his gun.

'Let's get goin' then,' Walters said.

'I'm going down to the emporium. I shouldn't be too long,' Gilby called to Mike.

They walked out on to the sidewalk, and Gilby was suddenly aware of Walters becoming more and more agitated as they saw the sign over the emporium. The man was clenching and unclenching his hand as he walked. Walters seemed to be practically running.

Through the window, Gilby could see the Tollivers getting ready to go out.

They came to the door, and out into the street. Jack Tolliver's face turned white as he saw Walters.

'No, Jess,' he yelled, holding out his hand to fend off something.

From the corner of his eye, Gilby saw Walters reaching for his gun.

He tried to stretch across to grab his hand, but as he did so a couple of kids came running round the corner and crashed into him, hurling him into the gutter A second later, he heard two shots and a couple of screams.

As he picked himself up, he saw Jess Walters with a smoking gun in his hand. The Tollivers lay on the ground, blood coming out of their chests. He grabbed the gun from Walters, and thrust it into his own belt. The two kids were looking at the bodies with the fascination of those who had seen violent death for the first time.

'Somebody get the undertaker,' he shouted, to anybody who was listening.

Gilby took hold of Walters' shoulder. Walters went along like a rag doll with all the stuffing knocked out of it.

Back at the office, Mike had locked the prisoners up. Gilby pushed Walters into a chair.

'Just what the hell was that about?' he snapped 'You're a lawman.'

'They're both killers,' Walters replied dully, his voice dry.

'That's not for us to say,' Gilby snapped again.

'It is for me to say,' Walters spoke slowly. 'He was my brother. Jack

Walters. She was Elizabeth Reynolds. She came to live in Chantry. The minute she saw him she went after him.'

'What's that got to do with it?' Gilby leaned across the desk, his voice tight and angry.

'He was a good man, 'til she got her hook into him. Didn't know too much about women.' Walters was leaning forward, his head slumped, his linked hands twisting. 'We all tried to tell him, but he wouldn't listen. Ma tried, Pa tried and my sister. Elizabeth Reynolds had him just where she wanted him.' For a moment Walters stopped speaking.

'And,' Gilby helped him.

'Pa had a prosperous lumber business, and she got him to take what was in the safe.' Walters looked at his feet, his voice breaking.

'When pay day came and there was nothing there, the lumberjacks found out and burned the place down. Pa was inside. The lumberjacks wouldn't let him get out. They killed him and that killed Ma.'

Gilby stared at Walters. 'You still had no right to commit murder,' he said, controlling his temper.

Both men were silent. Gilby watched the man's face working and the sweat beading out on it. He had lost all his ruddy colour, and was pasty white. His shoulders were shaking.

'You were a lawman,' Gilby said, getting up out of the chair. He crossed to where the pale-faced Walters was sitting, and tore the star off his vest.

'Lock him up, Mike,' he told the deputy. 'But don't tell them fellas he was a lawman, or they'll kill him.'

When Mike came back, Gilby handed him a sheet of paper.

'Get this wire off to Chantry. It'll tell them they need a new sheriff.' Gilby said flatly.

The stage robbery had been accomplished by an old woman. Twine Fourch had never heard of a female being a highway robber before. He followed the trail all the way to a dilapidated log cabin up Stone Mountain. What happened after that no one could believe even after townsmen from Jefferson found the old log house and the skeletal dying old woman. But before the mystery could be solved there would be two unnecessary killings, a bizarre suicide and a lynching.

GUNS OF THE GAMBLER

M. Duggan

Destitute gambler Ben Crow arrives in Mallory keen to claim his inheritance, only to discover that rancher Edward Bacon has other ideas. Set up by Miss Dorothy, who had fooled him completely, Ben finds himself dangling on the end of a rope. Saved from death, Ben sets off in pursuit of Miss Dorothy, determined upon retribution. However, his quest for vengeance turns into a rescue mission when she is kidnapped by a crazy man-burning bandit.

SIDEWINDER

John Dyson

All Flynn wants is to be Marshal of Tucson, but he is framed by the territory's richest rancher, Frank Buchanan, and thrown into Yuma prison. Five years later Flynn comes out, intent on clearing his name and burning for vengeance. Fists thud, knives flash and bullets fly as he rides both sides of the law and participates in kidnapping and double-dealing. He is once again arrested for a murder of which he is innocent. Can he escape the noose a second time?

SEVEN HELLS AND A SIXGUN

Jack Greer

Jim Cayman had been warned about Daphne Rankin, his boss's wife, and her little ways. When Daphne made a play for Jim and he resisted, the result was painful and about what he had feared. But suddenly matters went beyond the expected and he found himself left to die an awful death. Only then did he realise that there was far more than a woman scorned. He vowed that if he could escape from the hell-hole he would surely solve the mystery — and settle some scores.

THE BLOODING OF JETHRO

Frank Fields

When Jethro Smith's family is murdered by outlaws, vengeance is the one thing on his mind. He meets the brother of one of the murderers, who attempts to exploit Jethro's grudge in the pursuit of his own vendetta. The local preacher, formerly a sheriff, teaches Jethro how to use a gun. With his new-found skills, Jethro and his somewhat unwelcome friend pit themselves against seemingly impossible odds. Whatever the outcome lead would surely fly.